PETROLEUM MAN

PETROLEUM

MAN

A NOVEL

STANLEY CRAWFORD

THE OVERLOOK PRESS
WOODSTOCK & NEW YORK

The author wishes to express his gratitude for a Lila Wallace Reader's Digest Writing Award during the term of which this work was composed.

First published in the United States in 2005 by
The Overlook Press, Peter Mayer Publishers, Inc.
Woodstock & New York

WOODSTOCK:
One Overlook Drive
Woodstock, NY 12498
www.overlookpress.com
[for individual orders, bulk and special sales, contact our Woodstock office]

NEW YORK:
141 Wooster Street
New York, NY 10012

∞The paper used in this book meets the requirements for paper permanence as described in the ANSI Z39.48-1992 standard.

Cataloging-in-Publication Data is available from the Library of Congress

Book design and type formatting by Bernard Schleifer
Manufactured in the United States of America
FIRST EDITION
ISBN 1-58567-557-1
10 9 8 7 6 5 4 3 2 1

for Michael Ventura

PETROLEUM MAN

1. 1:24 SCALE 1934 FORD SEDAN

YOU ARE BOTH TOO YOUNG, FABIAN AND ROWENA, TO realize that this 1:24 scale plastic model is to be the first in a collection composing some thirty items altogether. Indeed, the concept collection is still probably beyond you, although if you look around the house of your parents—well, perhaps a better example would be to look around the house of us your grandparents—and pay attention to that moment when your sticky grasping hands approach some bright object and you hear the words, Look but don't touch, Fabian, which indicates that your still poorly coordinated grasp is threatening to close in on an item of one of my collections, a valuable object either fragile, because made of glass, or scratchable, because made of silver or gold or even brass or pewter, or needing to be handled with the greatest of care, because of the incredible sharpness of a blade, for example, or because of the remote possibility of the thing going off in your hands. That's what collections are, my little ones. They are things you do not touch until you have reached the age at which you can be fully trusted and are willing to assume responsibility in the event of breakage or some other form of degradation surely to cause a reduction in value in a collectible.

The 1:24 scale replicas I have bestowed on each of you as the first item in your future collections are, for you, briefly touchable but only under the supervision of your parents, which I have made abundantly clear to them. "1:24 scale" means that each inch of your model represents twenty-four inches in the original real full-sized vehicle. As very young children you two are 1:3 and 1:4 scale adults, as it were, by height. I intend to bestow these models on you every three to six months on the usual holidays, family birthdays, and various corporate milestone dates over the next decade or so, bringing your collection current with what will then be reality, by which time I expect I will have owned some thirty or forty different types of cars. Assembly of the complete collection will come, in short, during your fourteenth or fifteenth year, Fabian, and your twelfth or thirteenth, Rowena, and more precisely, God willing, on the occasion of that birthday of mine I have come to think of as the "big one." At that time I will have also completed these reflections on the real full-sized cars upon which the models are based, to be jotted down in my private 737 on my frequent business trips, during the early morning hours when the rest of the world is sound asleep 30,000 feet below. Or, at this very moment, 19,000 feet, as we are beginning our descent toward O'Hare. My steward has brought a message from the captain to the effect we'll be passing through some turbulence about five minutes before touchdown. At any rate, when you have attained the age of mature understanding, I will present both of you copies of this personal guide to your collections, suitably bound in leather. Or my estate will.

The models are yours, but under the provisional custody of your parents, and in turn under my custody, as the custodian of last resort. I have liberally coached your parents in the manner in which these accurate scale models can be handled, when taken down from the top of the bookshelves where they are to be displayed at all other times, and the manner in which they are to be extracted from their little plastic cases, and how your fingertips cleaned in advance will be allowed to touch them lightly, as your parents run them back and forth on smooth surfaces with their hands, while teaching you how to make appropriate car noises, which the dignity of my age no longer permits. I have of course already spoken words to this effect and was thoroughly charmed at the rapt way, mouths open, you stared up at me throughout, curled up on your parents' sofa.

The specific scale model, you are too young yet to appreciate, is far too glittery with plasticized chrome. I have communicated with the manufacturer about this. Nor were whitewall tires all that common back in the dark ages when many roads were still unpaved, which I will explain at a later date. But other details are reasonably accurate and more or less within scale. When literacy turns on its lights within your still tiny 1:24 scale brains, in about three years, if I have anything to do with it, you will notice that the raised letters on the underside indicate that these scale models were manufactured in a miserable tropical country, which you will surely never have to visit, in order to pump up the value of the shares your parents may or may not have in their portfolio but which I certainly have in mine, along with countless other investments which will assure you and your children and grandchildren a life of comfort and ease.

But I stray. This black 1934 Ford V-8 Sedan was not my first car, Fabian and Rowena, but is associated with my very first memory as a child of your age or perhaps a year or two younger. It is of no consequence, this memory, except to me. I was left alone in a mountain picnic ground banging away on aluminum pots and pans when I suddenly realized I was all alone among the pine trees, sitting in the fine sandy dirt next to the long dusty black sedan with red wire wheels, a silver stream babbling down below, along which ran a pair of railroad tracks where sooty steam engines puffed by every hour or so. To my eternal shame I burst into tears and began howling—of no consequence at all, this unfortunate episode, except that as a result I resolved, when I reached the age of being able to make resolves, to display signs of weakness or panic never again.

My point is this, my little ones. Your first memory, which is what you are now beginning to create, will affect the rest of your entire life—concepts, I know, still foreign to you: life, entire life, rest of entire life, and so on—but which I mention in order to alert you to the need, sooner or later, to select very carefully your very first memory for use later in your life.

Who knows? It may even be that moment when I pressed my face close to yours on the sofa and pulled the little plastic cases out of the gift bag and handed them to you simultaneously so as not to trigger any sibling rivalry, or any more of it. Or else that moment when you, Rowena, began squealing and banging your model against Fabian's, threatening to crack the plastic, and I gently pulled them away from both of your hands and took them off to your rooms and placed them high on the shelves above your beds. Perhaps that will be your first memory of your grandfather.

I would be honored, of course.

2. 1:24 SCALE 1939 FORD FORDOR SEDAN

YOUR GREAT-GRANDPARENTS WERE FRUGAL PEOPLE who bought cars only every five to ten years, unlike the son-in-law the universe has bizarrely chosen to torment me with and who seems to be perpetually shopping for cars, in a misguided attempt to curry my favor. His bulbous forehead is already beginning to show in yours, Rowena, a worrisome sign. You have no doubt heard the terms *Republican* and *democrat* and will soon be staring wide-eyed at various relations in the family and friends who walk in the door, attempting to see differences which are in fact quite invisible. What you should know, even before you can intellectually or emotionally grasp these differences, is that the frugality and generally virtuous comportment of your great-grandparents, who of course were my parents, were deeply marred by the fact of their being *liberal democrats* and voting for Roosevelt, Truman, and Kennedy. No doubt had they lived long enough they would have voted for those other three whose names will never cross my lips. It is also one of the closest held family secrets that your great-grandfather was a card-carrying member of the South Bend local of the metal fabricator's union, to my perpetual shame. Your father of course pretends to be a *liberal democrat* in order to annoy me, as are no doubt a few, a very few, of his colleagues in the investment banking law firm where he and your mother have tapped into another fountain of eternal wealth. Your mother, my daughter, is a staunch *Conservative Republican,* which I trust she used to make clear every time she changed your diapers. Without her principles, your father would have talked her into flushing you both down the toilet a long time ago.

At this early age, that is all you need to know about *Republicans* and *democrats.* Despite the odds, my *liberal democrat* parents gave birth to me—inconceivable as it may seem that a man as trim and controlled and disciplined and organized as me, whom you are fortunate to have as your grandfather, was ejected into the world via the usual messy birth canal and was able to recover from the experience and eventually amount to more than everyone else in my generation.

The green 1:24 scale 1939 Ford V-8 Fordor Sedan that I present to you each, Fabian and Rowena, on the occasion of my birthday, was a vehicle crucial to my successful life journey. "Fordor" is not a spelling mistake: it was Ford's way of saying "four-door." Corporations, my little ones, can spell any way they like, given their size, which you should not construe as license to spell any way *you* like, when the time comes for you to learn how to write in the next few years. At any rate, from its back seat I witnessed the first stages of the triumph of the automobile over all other forms of conveyance, notably streetcars and passenger trains, whose rails

were being dramatically ripped from the streets of our cities
as I came of age. I was filled with joy and a sense of triumph
as the sharp nose of our family Ford cleaved through crowds
of benighted pedestrians, our tires free at last of those
moments of uncertain traction on the slippery streetcar
tracks, so quickly paved over.

As in most things my *liberal democrat* parents were confused. You will notice identical signs in your father. Not my
first memory, I have instructed you in that, but my second or
third is of being read to by my well-meaning mother,
attempting to indoctrinate me in the virtues of rail travel by
putting me to sleep each night with "The Little Engine that
Could." Fortunately you will never have to undergo this
experience. Eventually I put a stop to the practice by removing the book one afternoon to a hiding place I had developed
in among some holly bushes on the north side of the garage
wall, where I proceeded to cut out all of the images of the
"little engine." I left them on the damp ground for their inks
to fade and for the paper to rot away, though I was careful to
return my mother's scissors to the kitchen drawer. I tell you
this only to suggest that should your father take to reading
you texts that make you uncomfortable in any way, I would
turn a blind eye to your making them disappear.

My father on the other hand held a more correct view,
despite his union membership, as evidenced by the manner
in which he kept a handwritten list in pencil, on a long sheet
of cardboard tacked to the rough wooden boards of the
garage wall, above his mechanic's workbench, in among
dozens of tattered and faded pinups torn from the pages of

certain magazines. The list was of streetcar lines and interurban rail systems which had been abandoned or had gone bankrupt, and each time he read of a new one in the newspaper, he scribbled its name on the cardboard. As a young boy himself once, he had been shouted at by a streetcar motorman on the Cottage Grove line in Chicago, causing him to wet his pants before an assembled audience of passengers—reason enough to become a pioneering proponent of the private automobile.

When you are a little older, Fabian, I will explain to you the meaning of the pinups, of which I obtained only the most shadowy of glimpses while being herded in and out of the darkened garage by my mother, often with a towel over my head.

But more important, it was toward the end of the era of the 1939 Ford Fordor Sedan that I began my career as an inventor, eventually successful beyond precedent, at least in terms of financial recognition. At age nine I devised a coin-operated chewing gum machine made out of a shoe box, balsa wood, pins, and tape. This ingenious machine, which I attached to a stand just inside the living room door, earned a profit of 500 percent from various visitors to the house who feared, from rumors I spread, that if they failed to buy a stick of gum on the way into the house and on the way out as well, they might well find one of their tires flat in the driveway. The original machine, my first invention, has miraculously survived in working order. It is on display in the new wing of the Manor in that full-scale re-creation of my Indiana boyhood room where now and then I demonstrate its

workings to visitors and journalists and explain how it was
my first and best instructor in the ways of capitalism.

I have composed these words in the air as usual, in
the wee hours when everyone else needs to sleep, on the
way to Taipei, after a first viewing of the fifteen-minute
video I took of you two unwrapping the gift boxes for the
1939 Ford Fordor models—after much fussing by the captain to get the wide-screen projection TV to work. *Next
time test it on the ground,* I snapped. Which only made my
chief steward drop the remote. Finally the co-pilot came
down from the flight deck and got the tape to play. A lovely scene, you two in your bunny pajamas and your little
bunny rabbit slippers on the sofa, so excited to see what
was in the boxes, one of those happy evenings when your
father had to stay late at the office. Your blue eyes were
open wide with expectation, Rowena, though yours were a
little shifty under your dark fluttering lashes, Fabian, perhaps resisting your mother's whisperings into your ear
about how to open the box.

And your little piping chorus, prompted by your mother,
I know, but who cares: *Thank you Grandpa!*

Fortunately you two missed your father's incredulous
and sarcastic remarks regarding my commendable efforts
when he arrived home late from the firm. This, after you had
been sent to bed with your new 1:24 scale Ford Fordors
safely installed on their shelves. I was simply—and generously—attempting to explain yet one more time my inten-

tions in creating these collections of model cars for my only grandchildren. I thought this a courtesy I owed my son-in-law despite his *liberal democrat* inclinations and despite my impression that we had already covered this ground a month or two ago when I first announced my plan.

Because, I was saying, *the cars I have owned over a period of many decades, including of course the strong association I had with my own parents' cars, starting with the most ordinary Fords and ending with the best vehicles money can buy, over a period of many decades—because a collection of these models is the best possible record of my trajectory from humble beginnings to stellar success. It's as simple as that.*

You had some early help from the Delahunt fortune, of course, he could not resist observing between mouthfuls of his prime rib as the rest of us sat around the table sipping our brandies.

A fraction less than you might think. Far, far less than the help you and Deedums have received from me, I corrected. And will receive upon my death, if you manage to behave yourself until then. An unlikely event, I would wager. Though this I did not say.

But model cars? I still don't see the point. Why not your old socks, presented in historical order...?

Chip, your mother wisely intervened.

Or bathmats. Or copies of the briefs filed against your corporations?

This is hardly necessary, Chip, your mother insisted.

He quaffed down half a glass of red wine and shrugged. *So we can look forward to these little family events for the next several years?*

You don't need to look forward to anything, Chippo. I'm doing this for my grandchildren, who happen to be your children.

He shot a steely look at your mother and asked: *And you approve?*

At which moment your grandmother Deirdre came downstairs from having read you two your bedtime stories and called out to me in her melodious voice as she entered the dining room, *Oh Fabian and Rowena just love those little cars you gave them, Leon.*

Whereupon I stood up and said my plane would be ready in forty minutes. *Taipei again,* I added and excused myself quickly enough to cross the room before wiping a tear from my eye at Deirdre's rare words of encouragement.

3. 1:24 SCALE 1949 FORD TUDOR SIX

I T WAS OF COURSE A BAD IDEA, I FREELY ADMIT, TO TRY to present you both 1:24 scale models of the 1949 Ford Tudor Six on the occasion, Fabian, of your fourth birthday, while you were both riding in the back seat. I thought I had activated the switch that blocks the operation of the rear windows. It was probably your grandmother Deirdre who had switched it off. She has the unfortunate habit of climbing in the car and starting it and then randomly, for all I can make out, pressing every button she can find on the door and dashboard as she drives away, windows half down, power mirrors askew, lights on, radio blaring, wipers waving, security system causing waterfowl to lift off from the lake. Of course it's always worse when she uses one of my cars.

In any event, Fabian, you are very, very lucky. Lucky that the driver of the car slowly passing ours was looking the other way when you hurled your Ford Tudor pot-metal model out the window into full rush-hour traffic. As far as I could see out the corner of my eye, it bounced off the windshield of the car next to us and then ricocheted across the concrete divider curb on to the hood of an exceedingly shiny lowrider which, as a singularly egregious form of automotive bastardization, deserved every inch of the long scratch your 1949 Ford Tudor probably inscribed on its hood. It is likely that the two drivers exchanged looks and hand gestures, which led to an illegal U-turn by the lowrider and then, at least from what I could make out, a high speed chase. You missed the exciting details of this episode, Fabian, because you were trying to wrest the other 1949 Ford Tudor from your little sister Rowena, forcing your grandmother Deirdre to unfasten her seatbelt with such violence that the buckle went flying and actually cracked—I realized only later—the windshield just below the upper-right-hand corner. The expense of this repair, considerable because the new glass has to be flown in from Germany, will be deducted from your share of my estate, Fabian. But belt unfastened, Deirdre was able to turn around and retrieve at least one of the offending presents, now safely installed atop Rowena's bookcase.

In your old age you will come to lament the lacuna in your collection, Fabian, although I have had the foresight to maintain privately within a secret recess of my study duplicate collections which you and your sister will have the good fortune to come across in your maturity, thus finding, miracle of miracle, the early lacks—and there will be more, I am sure—restored, as in some fairy tale. Nor did I tell you that the next day I returned to the four-lane boulevard in question, not a part of town we normally drive through but we knew no other way to put a stop to your tantrums, set off by your father's malign suggestion that your grandmother and I take you to a circus—and overcoming scruples about being in a less than savory part of town without bodyguards. Though, true, I must now and then slip away to live a little, incognito. At any rate, I returned to the boulevard and parked the car on the off chance that I might find the remains of the 1949 Ford Tudor (the name of the color is sea-mist green, by the way). To my astonishment, I was lucky. There, in the north-bound fast lane exactly where the lowrider had made its illegal U-turn, lay the flattened, shiny, paintless, and wheeless form of the 1949 Ford Tudor embedded in the asphalt. Awaiting a gap in the traffic occasioned by signal changes, I extracted my Swiss Army knife and selected a wide screwdriver blade and then ran across to the fast lane and with a swooping gesture pried up the flattened pot-metal shape and darted back to the curb in the nick of time, no small feat for a man of my advanced age with an unsteady left knee. I will never confide to anyone how close I came to being run over by a beer truck whose driver apparently seized upon my courageous act as an opportunity for sport. Although I could allow myself a brief chuckle upon regaining the curb, squashed model in hand, at the thought of the beer truck driver's reaction when he was told just who he had run down. Leon Tuggs, no less. *The* Leon Tuggs. The squashed model you will eventually discover in the shadow collection I maintain in my study.

Lest you think you are the only hell-raiser in the family I will reassure you by reporting that at your age or slightly older I was given a large red pot-metal toy car by my mother.

In a fit of pique—I wanted a fancier model with a working spring-suspension system—I took it out to the back yard one afternoon and pounded it flat with a brick and buried it under an apple tree. I tell you this so you will know that I was not perfect in my youth, even though I have conveyed the impression ever since.

4. 1:24 SCALE 1952 FORD F-100 PICKUP

OWING TO THE UNFORTUNATE EPISODE WITH THE LAST model three months ago, I surreptitiously placed the fourth model of your collection on top of your bookcases without announcing the fact, on a certain holiday, though of course I then waited breathlessly for a day and then a week and then *two months* for either of you to notice the new addition to your collections, during which time I had flown to Europe three times, Los Angeles six times, and twice to Asia. I write these words as usual on a night flight back from a frankly disastrous business meeting in Kuala Lumpur. The captain tells me the forest fires below are on Borneo. At any rate, for your eventual alertness, Rowena, you have earned points toward a bonus model. And I confess to being surprised. Between your grandmother's and your mother's efforts, your room has been filled with drifts of stuffed animals some four and five deep, some three hundred in number.

Now of course I entirely realize that you two are being raised not in an era of dearth and want as I was, in an era following on a previous era of even greater dearth and want, but instead you are living in a household of gluttonous consumption, as fueled by the huge bonuses of your lawyer parents plus your mother's share of my exponentially successful efforts. The labor of incorporating all these new toys and possessions into your still undeveloped psyches must be at times overwhelming. I have particularly talked to Deedums, which is what we call your mother but you are not to, and tried to explain to her that by giving you two everything you want within nanoseconds of your expressing interest, she may be corrupting one of the great principles of civilization itself. I can see nothing good, Fabian, coming of how your father has managed to fill your room with hard and soft dinosaurs of all shapes and sizes picked up on his travels— and you should know that two years ago I questioned, Rowena, the wisdom of building for you, at age three, a little suburb of dollhouses, seven at last count, on the Astroturf beyond the south deck. Deferred gratification, my little ones, is when you postpone doing something as long as you possibly can in order to give the weight of your postponing to the final possession of the object, to make the getting worth the wanting, owing to the poverty of just getting without any wanting at all.

Perhaps we deferred a little too much when we were your mother's young parents, being obliged by circumstances to maintain at least the appearances of a Spartan lifestyle. Be that as it may, the point of all this, especially for you, Fabian, is that destroying things is a way to replace the missing wanting, because you didn't have time to do any wanting beforehand. Upon destruction of the object in question, there then follows a period of lacking and finally wanting, regretfully, the thing destroyed, which, since it is destroyed—thrown out the window of a moving car, pounded flat out in the back yard—will thereafter forever be wanted and longed for and pined after.

In the future I shall make a point of displaying beforehand photographs of future models so that you can begin practicing wanting them well in advance. Deferred gratification builds character. The more gratification you can defer, the stronger your character. Which your mother understands but does not practice. Which your father neither understands nor practices.

But Rowena, lest you think you have got off scot-free, it took no great mental exertion to connect the 1:24 scale model of the fire-engine red 1952 Ford F-100 pickup missing from the top of your bookshelf—though I am puzzled here, as you are too young and too short to stand on a chair yet or haul a ladder up from the basement—with the corroded, paintless shape I trod on in the shallow end of the swimming pool, badly bruising my instep. There goes your bonus, Rowena. And now you too, like your brother, have a lacuna in your collection.

I hope you both know I am very close to rescinding the whole idea of the collection, through your failure to appreciate and respect the importance of my life, through models of the cars that were part of it. Your parents, by bestowing on you truckloads of toys in order to make up for their always being away amassing their own fortunes, may also be trying to undermine or bury my own efforts on your behalf.

Is it of no interest at all that the 1949 sea-mist green Ford Tudor was the car I learned to drive on or that the 1952 Ford F-100 pickup was the one in which I slid across the slippery brown leatherette seat to bestow my first kiss upon the heavily rouged cheek of my first girlfriend, who in panic accidentally unlatched the door and almost fell out on the her parents' driveway? They were poorly designed, those doors. You always had to open them and slam them hard whenever you went over a dip. She later became a lesbian.

Of course you're too young. You may always be too young.

5. 1:18 SCALE 1954 VOLKSWAGEN SUNROOF

I AM FULLY AWARE THAT IT IS IMPROPER FOR A GRAND-
father to expose his barely conscious grandchildren
to tales of his youthful sexual peccadilloes even though
someone, certainly not me, should eventually inform you of
the fact that your mother Deedums was already three
months pregnant with you, Fabian, when she unfortunately
convinced your father, who is assuredly but regrettably your
father, Craddock "Chip" Hoch, to marry her—or rather put
me in the excruciating position of offering to pay for the last
year remaining in the most expensive law school in the
nation if he would do the decent thing and preserve the
honor of your mother's family however little he seemed to
value that of his own, citing in the heat of the argument the
case of his half-sister—you see, it goes back quite a ways
with those *liberal democrats*—that she was quite happy raising
two toddlers without the benefit of wedlock. The Pittsburgh
branch of the Hoch family has lamentably fallen into *liberal
democrat* tendencies. True, I was being excessive when I
shouted, slamming books down on each other in my study,
that *Not getting married is not an option in the Tuggs family.*

Divorce is not an option for any Tuggs. The only option in this family is wedlock. Do you hear? Wedlock, young man, wedlock and going so far as to suggest that we had special ways, within the family, of making errant spouses disappear. *People drown all the time, operations fail, planes crash*—well, I was going too far, no doubt. But he agreed. I understood later that he threw the phone book in the general direction of your mother and stalked out of our guest suite saying, *Invite them all for all I care* or something like that. Five hundred and nineteen people showed up, plus bride, groom, and you, Fabian, *in utero*, making five hundred and twenty-one, at a cost of $203.95 per guest. Two thirds of the guests, being utterly unknown to me, appeared crazed with thirst and hunger and wearing clothes hastily pulled from the racks of thrift shops on the way from the airport. You, Fabian, probably had the best time, inside Deedum's tum-tum. Our accountants worked like slaves to get it classified as a charitable donation to the homeless. And the cost of the spa where your grandmother secretly underwent psychiatric treatment for three weeks, as a health expense. And the Tahitian honeymoon which your father extracted as a last-minute down-to-the-wire concession, as a business expense. Which added another fourteen percent to the cost, even so. You didn't come cheap, little ones.

Such has been the rush of events, Fabian, that I have only now, two days later, after a quick trip to Rome, come to understand what I glimpsed out the right rear window of the car just before your grandmother and I began to drive away from your parents' house. At first I made no connection between your shifty-eyed behavior and truncated odd little gestures toward your little sister standing next to you beside the car and the blood-curdling screams that emerged a few seconds later from her mouth. I halted the car immediately and jumped out and rushed around to the other side with your mother Deedums moaning and your father shouting at me for some reason, *Stop the car you fool!* We came upon the puzzling scene. He then changed his tune to *Move the car, move the car,* happily omitting the *you fool* bit. *Oh my god* your grandmother was screaming, *do something!* You were standing next to your sister with your hands in your pockets and rocking back and forth as if you had absolutely nothing to do with the fact that the bunny head of her left bunny-rabbit slipper was under the right rear tire of the Mercedes. I was about to rush around to get back in the car to move it off the slipper and therefore off Rowena's toes, we all supposed, when she simply removed her bare foot from the slipper, though still screaming and crying.

Are you hurt? Where does it hurt? Deedums said, crouching down and cradling her.

No but it's all crushed, she sobbed, *my bunny slipper.* And then muttered something into her mother's neck. Am I right, Fabian, in guessing that it was something like, *Fabian made me do it . . . ?*

Get the damned car off the slipper, will you, your father attempted to order.

A few things have been made clear by this little prank, Fabian. One, your father was at last able to speak his mind freely, voicing his opinion of his father-in-law, though this is probably the last time in his life he will have occasion to do that—or so I am to gather from the shouting that broke out between your parents just before they closed the front door on their way inside. And while, on reflection, I could possibly be pleased with your explorations of the nature of gravity and related forces, you should try to invent better experiments than egging on your sister to place the head of her bunny slipper under a tire of a 5000-pound car to *see what will happen*.

Though true, what has happened was very interesting. I will arrange a talk with your father at the earliest opportunity.

6. 1:24 SCALE 1955 OLDSMOBILE ROCKET 88 HARDTOP

WE'LL GET TO THAT ONE IN A MINUTE.

I feel it important to point out that the previous model, the 1:18 scale 1954 Volkswagen Sunroof, was far from cheap, with its doors and hood and sunroof that actually open and close—and will do so again if you are careful as you enter the age of manual dexterity, or at least as you are now doing, Fabian. You will notice sizes and therefore the scales of these models vary, which is owing to the capriciousness of model car manufacturers, though whenever possible I will order the larger size. For the Volkswagen's special metallic blue paint job, I had to call the factory—but that is a quaint, old-fashioned concept I must chase from my mind. Having chased quite a few factories abroad myself this past decade, with spectacular effects on the price of shares. At any rate, I had to call the customer service center, or whatever, which is probably located on Mars, and after being put on hold and forced to listen to music that sounded like elephants systematically breaking plate-glass windows— well, I turned it over to my secretary to deal with. To make a long story short, yes, for an exorbitant fee they could do a custom paint job and have the thing delivered in nine weeks, no doubt via several stops around the Indian subcontinent dodging labor unions.

By the same token, I suppose, there is no sense concealing from you, my little ones, what you can see with your own eyes when you go visit less fortunate playmates whose houses have only three bathrooms, not seven, and only two or three cars, not eight (or is it nine?), and only one swimming pool, not two, and no tennis courts, no skateboard ramps, no one-quarter scale dollhouse suburbs, and a much smaller army of illegal immigrants—but I ask, and indeed I posed this question to the President only the other night, how can a person be both "illegal" and an "immigrant"?—an army of such bruising your ears with bad English and probably worse Spanish. It is irrelevant whether I approve or disapprove of how your fiercely ambitious mother and dumb-luck father throw their children into the arms of this Central American Relief Society, which pumps a measurable portion of your inheritance south of the border each week—not to speak of the illicit portion—and charges it with the responsibility of feeding you and comforting you and playing with you except on those relatively rare occasions when your grandmother and I step in and restore a sense of normal *non-ethnic* family life.

Though true, your grandmother is a one-person ethnic group all her own. She comes from outer space. I have often thought. We met under the guiding principles of Murphy's Law, when her Renault wouldn't start on a damp morning in front of the women's dormitory, across from the campus green. Deirdre Delahunt. Nice dimples, good jaw, vague blue eyes, all of which you're probably going to get, Rowena, the Dayton Delahunt look, and nice body work. As I checked out all the wires in the rear engine compartment on my knees, struck by lust at first sight, I suggested that we go out on a date if I managed to fix it. A bad solenoid jumped with a screwdriver, and I had my date. It turned out that she had already heard of my legendary ability to fix things. She was attracted by my large powerful thighs. I have ordered that car for your collection—not the Renault, but the one we went out on our first date in. Yet another custom paint job. Within three years the damage was done. In the form of Deedums, your mother. Conceived in a rented garage on a rolling creeper with padded yellow upholstery underneath another car that will eventually enter your collections. But Tuggses don't divorce. We endure. Your grandmother and I have endured quite happily, considering, ever since. The garage? My agents were finally able to buy it last year.

Yes. I was trying to point out the obvious. You may not yet be able to imagine the thought so I will imagine it for you. You and your grandchildren and their children (this never stops, you see) will be richly endowed for centuries and centuries given the recent changes in the tax code and even better ones yet to come, as long as you practice sensible and legal birth control methods. You may have noticed, or very soon will, that often when there are many people sitting around the dining room table dessert portions become quite small, particularly when Flora doesn't understand that she was to have prepared dessert for *seventy* not *seventeen*, so let that be a lesson. For those doped-up people staggering around outside on the overheated streets shouting that the world is coming to an end and that global warming and other such bugaboos are slowly bringing us to a boil, you will be taught at an early age now to turn up the air-conditioning, which you can easily afford to do.

I haven't explained this as well as I might but there will be other opportunities. This flight is getting bumpy, coming in for a landing at Rotterdam. Right on time at 3:28 A.M.

7. 1:24 SCALE 1957 FIAT 1100 TV CONVERTIBLE

THERE ARE THOSE IDIOTS WHO PROPOSE THAT WE MUST soon give up our cars and take to moving around the earth on roller skates or our hands and knees or worse. Whenever you encounter one of these haranguing and hectoring types, who will also be carrying on about non-renewable resources and global warming, I would suggest you reply by pointing out that talk is so cheap as to be perpetually renewable and so could be quite reliably used to fill mass-transit hot-air balloons.

Did I subscribe to such nonsense I should not of course have embarked on this project to bestow on you, Fabian and Rowena, scale models of all the cars I have driven and owned over the past many decades and by so doing creating false hopes that you too, in your time, will eventually know an experience equally rich and varied—if not more so, given your father's propensity to trade in cars the first time the gas gauge reads empty. *Better cars than women,* I admit to muttering within his hearing, and of course I should not report that I am certain I heard him mutter back, not quite under his breath, *But why not both?* I fear this is steamy stuff for your still tender, unformed ears, those soft pink little flowers, at this particular moment, though of course you will not be reading these words until, one, you can actually read, and two, the universe willing, I have determined that you are of the emotional age to comprehend, with mature compassion and understanding, the details of my life that I will here and there divulge in the course of these descriptions. Naturally this will be much after that scornful age—your grand-mother and I went through this with Deedums—when you say such things as *Yuck, I don't want to hear about some old per-son's personal life, horrible, old, musty, food stains dribbled down their front.* Which happily does not apply to either your grandmother or me, though I can't tell you how many times your father, thirty years younger, has greeted me in your bowling-alley size living room with a flash of his perfectly straight if small teeth and a glad hand shooting out and the other ready with a crippling blow to the back, all with his fly unzipped. His is a typical Hoch smile. If moray eels could smile, they would look like Hochs.

So given the eventual date of your reading of these words, many years from now as fully responsible adults, there is probably little danger in my divulging details of a personal life for my intended audience, who will have accu-mulated quite a little crop of their own by then. And given the press's outrageous invention of details of my life and spending habits. But time rushes along. In only a few years you will be enduring your first "sex education" course in third or fourth grade, if my experience is any guide to your own, although I hope with much better results. Owing to the unfortunate graphics of the film strip, a wretched form of technology, I became convinced for many years that little girls were equipped with little hoses that hung down in the same way little boys' nozzles hung down, and that making love (or whatever it was called at the time) was a matter of hooking them up like two garden hoses, admittedly not a very appealing prospect. May you be spared.

I go into much more detail on these matters in my *General Theory of Industrial Sex*, which posits, to skirt around the juicy bits, that civilization is based on the male piston and the female cylinder, the male bolt and the female nut, the male screw and the female wood or sheet metal or whatever is screwed, into, the nail and the nailee, the latch and the keeper, the keystone and the arch, the plug and the socket, the thread and the nipple, the drill and the bit, the shaft and the sleeve or bearing or bushing, and so on and so forth. In other words, if you care to look around anywhere at all, you are surrounded by mirrors of what your little parts are supposed to do: plug, unplug, insert, extract, drill, bounce up and down, and so on. At the appropriate time and place, of course, which is the tricky bit. As an engineer, I cannot help but notice what most people instinctively deny, which is that our lives take place amid the quite public copulatings of the parts of hundreds and even thousands of machines and devices which we use and which surround us on all sides. I first learned this lesson when I realized that the most exciting event of first grade was when I raised my hand and asked to be granted permission to go over to the end of the long bookshelf under the window and insert my yellow number two pencil into the mechanical pencil sharpener and crank away, secretly inhaling the fragrance of cedar shavings the machine was generating within its little chrome and plastic container. If such things still exist in schools anymore. Pencils, pencil sharpeners. Little worms of cedar shavings. But within a few weeks, Fabian, you will soon be able to report to me if first grade remains as exciting as it used to be.

These last three cars were the ones in which I learned to apply the principles of internal combustion engines to the operation of my own body during college and graduate school. It is easier with the top down. In the Fiat convertible, though the car was a mechanical disaster. Hence the rented garage, the lift, the creeper with yellow padding. The rest is history. The Oldsmobile was implicated in an earlier pre-Deirdre adventure with, shall we say, a professional female engineer intimately familiar with the principles of Industrial Sex and who for a modest fee would perform private demonstrations, under the blinking red light of a radio tower, where the inadequacy of my fourth-grade sex education course led me to misunderstand the options available. I was still thinking in terms of connecting garden hoses—having not yet learned to observe the world at hand much more closely, as I was soon to do particularly in repairing the for-ever-breaking-down Fiat.

This inept initiation took place in Calumet City, not far from Chicago, where my *liberal democrat* parents had shipped me off to a *communist university*, which shall deservedly remain nameless and which will see not one cent added to its endowment from the Tuggs fortune. My *General*

Theory of Industrial Sex is intended to spare future generations from ever having to experience again the sorts of unfortunate episodes I had to endure as a young man. Though in deference to your grandmother, I am withholding publication until my "big one," eight years hence.

8. 1:12 SCALE 1956 CITROËN 2CV SEDAN

FAMILY LORE, I AM CERTAIN, HAS ALREADY COLORFULLY distorted the turning point episode in my college studies in which I fled the *communist university* and its infamous *liberal arts program* at the end of my sophomore year for a much more down-to-earth university in southern Illinois. There I entered the engineering department and eventually became its most famous graduate of the latter part of the last century, if not all time. One of the great sadnesses of my career was that I made my fortune not from inventing a device based on what I call my principles of Industrial Sex but from one of those random brain waves that came during a warm bath, just as I was about to drowse off. In a flash of internal lightning the idea for the patent jolted me upright: one of those little things of paper which cost nothing to manufacture but which everyone is will to pay for. It warms the cockles of my heart every time someone activates its proprietary substance (which no one has yet succeeded in pirating) and a tenth of a cent is deposited in my account. This may not seem like much, my little ones, but multiply it by billions and billions on a good day and you will soon see where we can get with a mere tenth of a cent. And if you listen closely, you can hear the trees of the great forests crashing to the ground on the way to becoming all the little paper Thingies®*, which eventually add up to your grandfather being able to buy you yet another model for your collection, such as this gray 1:12 scale 1956 Citroën 2CV four-door sedan whose full scale equivalent I drove for two years while getting my engineering degree. A particularly fine model with opening doors and sunroof and hood and trunk lid, with removable seats. The standard scale model of this car is a much tarted up later edition. It cost me a pretty penny to have them make up the earlier plain-Jane version, gray and chromeless, which was far more common.

This car was something of a guilty hangover from my *communist university liberal arts* days. Cleverly engineered with only thirty-some moving parts, it was really a two-cylinder motorcycle enclosed in a tin-can of a body of anteater inspiration, with components easy to unbolt and unhitch. Top speed, about fifty miles per hour, tolerable in those years, at fifty miles a gallon. Much mocked by my fellow engineering students, who favored extravagant tanks from the early 1950s.

I soon bested them with my next car, as you will see in my addition to your collections to be made soon, in observance of the Fourth of July, which earned me induction into the secret Black Box Society, "Dedicated to screwing up the world with technology for fun and profit." No women, of course, have ever been inducted. And of course I have sworn in blood never to reveal the Black Box Society secret hand-

---

*Thingie® is a registered trademark of Thingie®-Gazillion International. Use with permission.

shake. I quickly rose within its ranks to become Omni-Potent Potentate and Grand Dragon. As required by the position I engineered a stunt in which two campus police cars were surreptitiously rewired to reverse their directional signals, causing much merriment around campus and the expulsion of my partner in crime, the Vice Omni-Potent Potentate, who was unable to hold his silence after twenty years. He claimed in a tabloid article that his expulsion had destroyed his future career and would have nipped mine in the bud too, had he confessed or had I been caught. He was always a poor sport, that one.

9. 1:18 SCALE 1933 PACKARD STRAIGHT EIGHT

YOU MAY HAVE STILL BEEN IN THE HALLWAY NEXT TO the dining room, I fear, my little ones, when I happened to suggest in a rather too loud voice to your father that there would very definitely be repercussions if he chose to go through with his plans to move out of Fairlawn-Fairview Lake Estates to an even larger house more than forty miles away in what he regards as a more fashionable part of Connecticut. All the more galling given the expense and trouble I went to in the first place in creating Fairlawn-Fairview Lake Estates on the edge of my own Fairlawn-Fairview Lake Manor, for the comfort and convenience of your parents and you, my grandchildren—and allowing them to buy the largest house on the largest tract to boot. What could possibly be lacking in the present arrangement—which includes nine bathrooms, seven hot tubs, five-bedroom guest house, servants' quarters, tennis courts, sauna, pool, guard house at the end of the drive, and its own dock on the lake. I know your father considers it a hardship to have to keep his yacht on the Sound, a ten-minute drive away, but a bit of suffering is good for the character.

Move more than ten miles away, old Chippo, and Deedums gets nothing, I advised loudly. *As in zero, nada, nyet. Absolutely nothing. The fifteen thousand square feet you have here is more than adequate, let alone the thirty-five acres.*

Your father had the gall to suggest that I was rarely at home within *this charmed circle ten miles in diameter*, to use his words, *so what the hell does it matter?*

It matters because I say it matters. And when I say it matters, it matters. It matters a thousand times more than anyone else saying it matters.

So you value me at approximately one-one-thousandth of your own self worth?

An excellent ratio, I bellowed, quaffing some more brandy, *for the relationship of father-in-law to son-in-law, Chip. Excellent. Congratulations. I'm pleased that at last you fully understand the numbers here.*

Whereupon your mother Deedums, having probably shooed you two upstairs, strode into the living room and asked what the matter was. On this, at least, your father and I were agreed. *Nothing*, we said in unison. Though I was irked that our altercation short-circuited my intention to trot upstairs and make certain your mother and your nanny had tucked you in properly and to catch a glimpse of your long silken blond hair, Rowena, spread out on the white pillow, and to wish you a last happy birthday for the day. I also wanted to check on the progress of the healing of your nose, Fabian, which you had skinned while crashing into the bushes with your latest bicycle. Given the somewhat tense relations between me and your father, I have put off bringing up the question of why he thinks it important for you to have so many bicycles, fifteen at last count. At age six, I only had one.

But I stray. The 1933 Packard Straight Eight, models of which I have given you both on the occasion of your fourth birthday, Rowena, was not quite yet an antique in 1961, just a tired, old, and inexpensive car. My fellow engineering students were impressed, however, by the car's dual sidemounts and its long, high nose, which indicated power and potency, and it gained me entry into the Black Box Society, becoming the Society's official if secret car during my one-year tenure as Omni-Potent Potentate and Grand Dragon. The car was bought new and owned by a steel-mill family who had successfully put down a union demonstration with no loss of life on the side of management. Its high hood, which shrouded the enormously long and deep straight-eight engine, was more than a third of the length of the long car. The copulating thrum of the long-stroke engine was a joy to hear and feel through the heavy steel of the body; it was, this sound, the inspiration, for one of the more brilliant theses of my *General Theory of Industrial Sex*, if I may say so myself.

10. 1:24 SCALE 1957 ROVER 75 FOUR DOOR SEDAN

BECAUSE IT WAS TO BE SOME YEARS BEFORE MY Thingie® patent, my seventh, I was obliged to settle for inexpensive back-of-the-lot used cars while I completed my graduate studies and slowly built up my engineering practice. And when the grand Packard—excellent off the shelf 1:18 scale model, I must say—turned out to require more time and patience than a young blade like me could spare, I sold it to a budding collector and for a song picked up a five-year-old Rover 75, whose 1:24 scale model I had to send to England for. A heavy car of restrained and somewhat blunt elegance known as the "poor man's Rolls-Royce," this one suffered from brakes that had to be pumped and an inoperative starter, which required me to hand crank it unless parked on a hill, and a noisy timing chain. Ah, but I think back fondly on this disreputable time of bad cars and heavy drinking with my fellow students and midnight equations and theories and raunchy conversations in the three-stall shower room in the dorm, which I have re-created in one of my galleries in the Manor using fixtures salvaged from a recent renovation of the actual dorm. It is one of those fully functional time capsules I can revisit whenever the whim strikes me, seeking to refresh my youthful soul—though I must be careful not to be overcome with nostalgia.

These were the days when I first elaborated my theory of Industrial Sex in a finally coherent form. I also anonymously published *The Steel Penis and the Iron Vagina*, expanding on material I could clearly not include in my thesis, "The Place of Tolerances in 18th-Century Metallurgy," which was the germ for my later survey, *A History of Tolerances*, still used as a pirated text at Bombay University, or so I am told. At the proper time in your lives, I will bestow signed copies of *Tolerances* on each of you, to give a certain weight and gravitas to your personal libraries.

At this time—I was in my mid-late twenties—I also developed a personal financial graphing system which has served me in good stead ever since. My only regret is that I did not start it at your ages, my little ones—or that that I did not have a well-meaning adult set it up for me, as like you I would not yet have been able to comprehend its subtleties and long-term benefits. Essentially the system consists of four line graphs recording the progress of my income, savings, and other liquid investments, real property, and debt load. At twenty-five, say, my debt load was rapidly rising under the burden of expenses exceeding income, my income appeared to be falling, my savings and investments (the cream 1957 Rover 75 four-door sedan worth $150, some pots and pans, some used furniture, a slide rule, etc.) were virtually nil, and I was without equity in real property whatsoever. Had there been any point at the time, a fifth line could have been added, projecting the potential value of future inheritances and the like, but as I say, there seemed to be no point, as my frugal *liberal democrat* parents were soon to have their modest assets stripped away from them by those inventive entrepreneurial strategies of the health care industry, which suggested, from another point of view, excellent investment opportunities.

At your age and in your circumstances, Fabian and Rowena, your graphs would look quite attractive and would be exceedingly pleasing to contemplate—they could be hung on the walls above your beds. There would be the steady green line of your weekly allowance, probably twice the value of my graduate school stipend; there would be no red line of debt; there would be the rising blue line of your trust funds, or lines, because you have two each, one from your parents, the low one, and one from your grandparents, the high one, about five hundred times higher; and the faint yellow lines of the estimated value of your twin inheritances, the highest of all, quite up there at the ceiling. It is so handy to have this financial material at your fingertips—or posted near your bed so that you can go to sleep and wake up able to reflect upon these essential realities of human existence. As in fact I have, continuously since my late twenties. Though now of course I use a satellite-fed digital projection system on a screen that drops from the ceiling at the foot of my bed, at the push of a button, and a similar arrangement in my personal 737.

Yet from your bedside graphs, Fabian and Rowena, all may not be quite as simple and rosy as it seems, for somewhere else in the world there will be children whose bedside graphs feature a blossoming red line of indebtedness and no asset lines at all. Probably, come to think of it, 29,000 feet directly below me in the dark, as I believe we are now passing over some part of Indonesia on the way to Bangkok. At any rate, from this you would need to gather—I will help here—that the chief difference between the rich and the poor is that the poor must borrow in order to survive, and the rich to lend in order to thrive. What we call stocks and bonds and mortgages and investments in general are those instruments by which the rich lend their money to those less rich, middling, or simply poor. For those people who wish to believe that a world is possible without extremes of grinding poverty—lamentable as they are—and without extremes of great wealth—admirable as they are too—I can only say that this would be a world in which there was only one sex, or only day and no night, only summer without winter, with people of all the same height, weight, and of the same intelligence. And so on. You can see what a boring place the world would become.

Things move and flow and reciprocate because *tolerances* permit them to do so. For *tolerances* read *differences*. Without tolerances, or differences, things jam, seize up, and freeze. Which will become perfectly clear when eventually you consult my various volumes on the subject.

A last word of reassurance, however. Poverty will be around as long as the need for wealth persists. And while the poor have proven quite well their ability to get by on nothing, we rich people would be quite lost without our wealth.

As you probably have guessed by now, your grandmother and I don't entirely agree on this. She has a fatal
weakness for the lost cause, for which I believe she mistook
me back in our student days of defective Chevys and Fiats.

But I for one am beginning to feel a little cramped in
the Manor's seventy-eight rooms, which is why I'm looking
forward to the day when the construction of the extension
of the new north wing, which will double the size of the
house, is finally complete. Deirdre has become so busy with
her so-called good works, however, I doubt she will hardly
notice—at least not until she gets lost.

My train of thought was interrupted by the captain
reporting an emergency on the main runway at Delhi, forcing us into a holding pattern for a tedious hour and a half,
but I have failed to recover a point I was going to make. Be
that as it may, I must say that I certainly enjoyed our afternoon yesterday out on the Cape, particularly after your
father had to excuse himself to fly back to the city to deal
with an unexpected court ruling. The weather even seemed
to improve after he left, the breeze dropped, and the afternoon turned warm and hazy, with you two digging holes and
building castles in the sand while the Atlantic rolled ponder-
ously beyond, your nimble bodies unmarked by time, and
your grandmother carrying on about her latest lost cause to
Deedums under the umbrella while I half dozed, having finished combing through the financial pages.

There came a moment just before we were to leave

when I could hardly restrain myself from thrusting myself up out of the beach chair and approaching you, Fabian, and squatting down and speaking the words over the sound of the surf—casually, as if I was only admiring your oddly unadventurous sand castle, which was more like a defensive bunker—softly speaking the words of the message I am at times so desperate to impart to you, that nugget of wisdom that could spare you so much grief and disappointment. But I knew, had I done so—had I actually stood up from my chair and crossed the warm sand to find myself at your side, your brown arms and back covered with a frosting of drying sand, I would have been rendered speechless in the sudden real-ization that I could never fit it all into so few words, in what surely would have been the briefest of moments.

11. 1:12 SCALE 1953 CHEVROLET BEL AIR CONVERTIBLE

THIS WAS THE CAR——A STOMACH-TURNING SHADE OF peanut-butter orange, with white top and trim—with which I courted and won your grandmother Deirdre, who to her credit did not conceal the fact that she would eventually be two-thirds of the Dayton, Ohio, KlampTite-MagicMastic fortune, on our third date. I bought the Chevy from a fellow engineer who desperately needed the $175 I had to borrow from yet another friend to buy it, for our first date, not expecting Deirdre (who I first thought was a mere student in anthropology) to be impressed by the wretched Rover's walnut and leather appointments while I was attempting to start it with a hand crank. Or to stop, once I got it running, with vigorous pumpings of the brake pedal while controlling its tendency to swerve sharply into incoming traffic whenever the brakes finally did engage. The Chevy started and stopped and ran sluggishly in between, with a soft almost opulent wallowing caused by inoperative shock absorbers, and if you kept the windows half open or the top down the smell of exhaust was not overpowering. There were spots on the front bench seat where you could sit without the cracked plastic upholstery working holes into your clothing. Happily Deirdre was into downward mobility.

I was not. My descent into penury was galling. It was as if I was being pushed back into the world of my too-thrifty parents. I calculated that the Chevy ran on the average thirty-one miles before needing to be repaired. Which only fueled, the correcting of its defects, your grandmother's ardor. Deirdre was the first and only young woman I knew for whom mechanical breakdown was an aphrodisiac. It was intense hormonal activation at first sight. Which I later came to think of as major misunderstanding at first sight.

Once, while I was on my knees replacing one bald tire with another one, slightly less bald, she called out from the front seat: *I love this. The simple life. I've never broken down in a car before.*

It was the first time I heard the phrase from her lips, *the simple life.*

Sure, I said to myself, *sure, we can find a bit of time for the simple life here and there in between bouts of conquering the world.*

Beware, my little pets, of those words that may be whispered as you lie arm in arm with your future partner on a rolling creeper with yellow plastic padding on a concrete floor in a dark garage underneath the greasy chassis of one of those cars that never seem to want to run. I even have thought of expunging this model from your collections, wiping a bit of history off the map, as it were, but my passion for historical accuracy has got the better of me.

It keeps coming back, that urgent feeling I had a month ago on the beach. Only now as I watch you playing on the

wine-red living room carpet, Fabian, on one of those happy
evenings when your father has to work late at the office, and
you push one of the models of your collection back and forth
on the exquisitely soft carpeting, its wheels making dew-like
marks in the nap of the wool, and you stare dreamily into its
little plastic windows, and hum little engine noises, a rooster of blond hair sticking up from your still narrow, flat little boy's head—no coiffeur has succeeded in taming it, a
Tuggs family trait—I often wonder what I could say to you
that would spare you all the grief with women that sooner or
later you too are bound to endure. What would be the message I would whisper into your ear some quiet evening?
What is the secret? You are my last chance to tell anyone the
truth while I still have it within my grasp. Yet you are still too
young, too receptively young.

But fortunately, my little ones, at least you live in a
world in which you have to fix nothing. There's an army of
people in the house and out there who will fix whatever
needs fixing or will simply throw it out and buy another
one. And fortunately long gone is the world in which heavy
glass bottles once containing soda pop, the food of the poor,
were laboriously lugged down a hot sidewalk to the corner
store where the grocer suspiciously paid back their deposit
in dimes and nickels and pennies. I tell you all this so that
you will not be tempted by some kind of *nostalgie de la boue*
when you come of age and seek to throw off the trappings
of hard-earned wealth and privilege in a mistaken quest for
a *simple life* of eating berries and nuts in the woods and
sleeping on the ground under boughs of pine needles—and

living off of deposit money from empty soda-pop bottles.

Your grandmother Deirdre is a perfect example of what happens when you try to escape your class through half-baked notions of the *simple life*. I was able to bring her back into the fold, or into her fold, which soon became mine. A deep misunderstanding was at the base of her delusions, I fear, and as result I have maintained a one-man war against the Internal Revenue Service, seeking the abolition of the term *unearned income* or, that failing, its revision into *deserved income*.

All income, my pets, is deserved—in the sense that at the end of the day I, or even you, at your tender ages, can readily work up a list of reasons why we deserve what we receive and what we possess. Such lists include the simple basics of *I am alive, and therefore I deserve,* as well as more refined items, such as my exquisite sense of taste that deserves to be satisfied, my pride of ownership, to a listing of all the good thoughts I have had all day and even the good deeds I have performed and will definitely perform in the future or will order someone to carry out in my name.

As for your grandmother, you know the story. The scrapbooks are still too often passed around the family gatherings when we're not there, I fear. How Deirdre and I eloped in the 1953 Chevy Bel Air convertible, how our disappearance sparked a nationwide woman-hunt, which lasted through the abrupt bankruptcy of KlampTite-MagicMastic —since become a classic textbook study of pioneering offshore outsourcing and diversification gone wrong. This historic event fortunately took over the front pages and caused the stories about Deirdre to sink into trivia with headlines such as *Investigators Fail to Link KlampTite-MagicMastic Heiress Disappearance with Bankruptcy.* And how we hid out for two weeks in the upper reaches of the Michigan woods on the grounds of a closed-up hunting lodge owned by one of her uncles, living on berries and trout, making vigorous love among the ferns and mosquitoes, developing abscesses and excessive flatulence—until finally she said to me in our damp molding connubial sleeping bag, *I would give anything for a warm bath. . . .* And I suggested, *There are as many warm baths as you want to take back in Ohio.*

Contrary to family lore, which I know is muttered back and forth among your parents' generation as they sniff and snort long after your grandmother and I have gone to bed, things about us being *hippies* and *anti-war protestors*—I will point out only that we were neither, we were simply an impecunious engineer and a somewhat diminished heiress who found a small-town minister to marry us on our way into the woods. Far more diminished than either of us could have imagined during our two-week attempt at the *simple life.* Had we waited until afterward, it would have been a far different story. But be that as it may, upon our emergence, there was only one warm bath, the night before the Delahunt mansion went on the block.

But it was a bath to rival that of Archimedes and his ancient *Eureka!*—if not exceed it, for owing to modern patent laws and our legal system, I was eventually able to reap the full benefits of my discovery of the Thingie® while Archimedes, without a patent attorney in sight, was unable to patent gunpowder, or was it gravity? Or whatever it was he thought up in the bath. I will have that looked up as soon as we touch down at O'Hare, in about two hours.

12. 1:24 SCALE 1960 MERCEDES-BENZ 190 4-DOOR SEDAN

IT IS FORTUNATE THAT YOU ARE STILL TOO YOUNG TO entirely understand the words spray painted last night on the walls of the main security gatehouse of Fairlawn-Fairview Lake Estates, the third such incident in the past two years—in fact you may not even recognize the graffiti as being offensive, having already practiced yourselves with magic markers on the expensive Florentine wallpaper that decorates both your rooms. The cost to efface these bold squiggles and scribbles—or rather whether to efface them at this time or leave them for family members and friends to *appreciate*—apparently set off one of those little disagreements between your father and my daughter that can go on for several days and reach far into the future, into what prep schools and universities you will attend and what kind of person you will marry and how, finally, you will deal with your own children when they take black markers to what is surely the most expensive wallpaper between here and Mars. In this one instance I would agree with your father. In just this one instance. Were I to be asked. Though I did take a few shots of the wallpaper with the little video

camera I normally reserve to record those moments when I
bestow the model cars on you.

Your still tender youth means that as yet I have no need
to explain the words EAT THE rICH splashed across the high
antiqued brick wall next the gatehouse where the security
guard was either criminally asleep or watching TV, other
than to observe that such thinking is the work of deranged
troublemakers suffering from chemical imbalances occasioned by dietary deficiencies brought on, in turn, by poor
lifestyle choices. You will surely have noticed, however, that
neither your grandmother or I, nor your parents—one of
the rare things all four of us actually agree about—allow
soda pop or so-called soft drinks into either of our houses,
on the grounds that such beverages are primarily manufactured to quench the thirst of the poor. By choosing such beverages you, or rather they, in this case, the poor, are also
choosing the negative health effects that such beverages
bring upon the individual body, and are therefore suffering
exactly what they deserve. This same flaw in human nature,
which so conveniently distinguishes poor from rich, also
makes investing in companies that produce such goods an
excellent financial strategy. Because of such investments, and
here is where my little ones need to prick up their ears, your
parents are easily able to afford those far more nutritious
beverages whose consumption will build strong bodies and
good teeth. Even the very young can often benefit from
good market advice—as I have been saying for much of my
adult life.

As for the car, a 1:24 scale black 1960 Mercedes-Benz

190 4-Door Sedan, on the occasion of Thanksgiving, Fabian
and Rowena, this was the well-used and somewhat clunky
vehicle which transported your grandmother and me ultimately to the evening bathtub session that eventually led to
the salvaging of the tattered remains of the KlampTite-
MagicMastic family fortune and its merging with the exponentially burgeoning Thingie® Corporation International, in
a nice admixture of dying old money and lively new cash.
While I lay limp and spent and dozing off, I languidly
explored some of the unsolved intricacies of my Theory of
Industrial Sex, in the bathwater whose temperature was
cooling owing to the evaporative heat loss of its surface, but
also being raised by the slow dribble of hot water from the
fixture. Deirdre was darting back and forth, in and out of
the bathroom, trying to raise my drooping lids with questions such as *Should I wear this?* and *Should I wear that?*, holding up fancy dresses for the last dinner in the old Delahunt
house, in the dining room downstairs. We were already fifteen minutes late, delayed by our little game with rubber
ducks and wooden sailing ships in the bath, and so on and so
forth. I was absently answering, *Yes, this* and *No, that other one*,
not really paying attention because deep within my mind I
was systematically inventing the famous Thingie® and thinking through the industrial processes by which it would be
manufactured and assembled and even packaged and the
multitude of uses to which it would be put—but minus the
one single thing that would make everything else work, the
special moistenable agent and several related polymer com-
pounds that it would take me another three years and count-

less baths to stumble on. Fortunately my agents were able to salvage most of the fixtures and much of the black and white tile from the third-floor bathroom of the Delahunt mansion before it was demolished, eventually providing the basis for an excellent reconstruction in one of the galleries of the Manor's north wing extension.

I am composing these words on a flight back from Bangkok, where I was delighted to find a company which will custom build models in 1:12 to 1:8 scale in any trim level or color, for a fraction of the cost of my previous suppliers, through a U.S. Government supported program for rehabilitating felons through building such models. Based on family photographs and approximate measurements, they will also be able to create scale models in cloth and plastic or rubber of us all to place inside the car models. They showed me some examples, and I pointed out that white people are white, not swarthy, and our noses are not *that* prominent— your father is an exception here, but he will not be modeled—and neither the Tuggs nor Delahunts are notable for dark bushy eyebrows. Apparently the program attracts felons of higher than average intelligence and education; such inmates, I was told, entertain fantasies about cars they will surely never be able to own, possibly never even see in real life, and this is the fuel that propels them in their exacting efforts, to your benefit, my pets, at one third the previous cost.

13. 1:12 SCALE 1966 VOLKSWAGEN WESTFALIA CAMPER VAN

LITTLE FABIAN, THE WORDS THAT FOLLOW ON THE occasion of your sixth birthday are for you only, as between man and man. Unfortunately because of bad weather over the North Atlantic the flight has been delayed six hours. I have decided to stay with the plane rather than try to get back to London for a couple of hours, in case the weather opens up earlier than planned. But at least this year I was actually able to attend your birthday party, for the first time in three years. Obviously what follows are things I could not have said to you face to face, video camera running, when I presented this model to you, an occasion which you rose to nicely with a sweet smile—thank god it looks like you will have good Delahunt teeth, not your father's small nippers—and a fluttering of your long eyelashes. But as I was saying, in terms of the genes we share in common, the many decades that separate us are but a few grains of sand on the whole of your favorite winter beaches on the Côte d'Azur, Cabo San Lucas, Bali, or even Florida. Your birthday car, by the way, with its as-usual expensive paint job—it will be six months before my new supplier kicks in—a light blue 1966 Volkswagen Westfalia Camper Van with operating pop-top and front and side sliding doors, and four miniature sleeping bags, was bought at Deirdre's insistence—the actual car, not the model, that is—when she began feeling the urge to head for the woods again and resume the *simple life,* though this time with a number of tools and simple appliances which she found in some catalogue and which she insisted on showing me on the sofa after dinner—well before you were born.

Look, she said, her blue eyes brightening, *with that we could make our own yogurt for little Deedums.*

I tried to keep my replies noncommittal. *Could we?*

Undaunted she licked her finger and continued leafing through the slick pages. *Bees! Beehives! We could make our own honey!*

Had she forgotten, I wondered, that a single bee sting can send me into a state of potentially fatal shock?

At any rate I managed to satisfy her urge to go back to the *simple life* through a series of uncomfortable camping trips to the upper reaches of Lake Michigan during seasons rich in insect life.

Bugs are at the heart of the simple life, my dear, I suggested on more than one occasion. *In fact the simple life is centered around those most simple of creatures, the bug. If there are no bugs, we are not living the simple life. Through their inconsiderate and even dangerous behavior, bugs may be trying to tell us that the simple life may not be what it is cracked up to be.*

What I feel you need to know, Fabian, is that I don't really understand women or for that matter actually like them, except possibly your five-year-old sister. And children in general seem to be another species entirely. This is an identifying mark, some would say affliction, of the engineering profession and other professions and trades that design, fabricate, cast, forge, bend, anneal, extrude, roll, stamp, and crush things out of metal and other hard substances, and additionally submit them to drilling, welding, bending, radiating, punching, embossing, grinding, buffing, polishing, plating, sandblasting, sawing, reaming, painting, and so on. In my experience all women abhor such processes and are quick to flee the premises in which greasy or sooty men pound on sheet metal with hammers, to use a crude example, or tighten huge bolts with mammoth wrenches or direct gushing hoses of odiferous chemicals into tanks and tanker trucks and tanker ships. Only men, not women, delight in devising explosives, poisons, projectiles, traps, machines, and weapons in general. *Name one weapon invented by a woman.* All this you should know as a young man, Fabian, so that as soon as you begin to feel those strictly masculine urges within you, you can begin to guide them toward those areas of male endeavor that will return the highest degree of delight and excitement over the long run.

What I don't understand about women is why they fail to understand, in turn, these essential male characteristics, even though at an early phase of a courting relationship they may *pretend* to admire the size of your car or *pretend* to share in your excitement at developing some revolutionary toxic substance that promises to rid the world of cockroaches at last, or they will *pretend* to admire your ability to bring down an obsolete fifty-story building with the pressing of a button—and so on. First they will pretend, and then, having got what they want, which I will not detail until you are a little older, they will turn their backs and lose complete interest in what you are doing as a *man* and even go so far as to hint that what you are doing is cold or childish or irrelevant or destructive of the so-called environment.

My advice here, young man, is that you should prepare yourself in advance for the double-bind the opposite sex will always trap you in. Whenever you find yourself deep in some manly activity in which you are testing your new strength and canny intelligence against metals, rocks, glass, wood, and other hard and/or toxic or dangerous materials, you should be aware of exactly why some young woman is egging you on to make that bigger and better bulldozer or that stronger and more potent poisonous gas or that bigger and better atom bomb. Go ahead and do it, is my advice, but with the firm knowledge that later you are sure to be accused of making a shambles of everything. The long and the short of it is that men *invent* the world while women only *populate* it.

Be that as it may, now that the last of your baby teeth has finally fallen out, coincidentally on your seventh birthday, your mother has been kind enough to supply me with the complete set, minus the two you misplaced at school, from which I am commissioning the construction of gleaming white marble replicas, which will measure approximately eighteen inches on a side, to be eventually housed in one of the small galleries of the new wing of the Manor.

Probably between the gallery of my collection of antique and foreign condom dispensing machines, which you will be admitted to at a more appropriate age, and the one for my collection of antique bolts and nuts, screws, nails, and corkscrews.

14. COMMEMORATIVE COLLECTOR'S SPECIAL EDITION OF *THE COMPREHENSIVE ENCYCLOPEDIA OF ALL THE WORLD'S CARS*

IN SHORT, MY LITTLE FABIAN, TO CONTINUE OUR discussion, now that I have got back in the air, a rare daytime flight to Rio de Janeiro during which business will have to wait—in short, men and women have almost nothing in common and you may wonder—especially given your father's behavior—why they bother to live together at all. In general, I now believe they shouldn't, or that at the very most they should live in separate houses on the same property, within a minimum distance of a hundred yards of each other, perhaps with a connubial tent in between—the sort of detail your grandmother would appreciate. She is fanatical about tents. I can never remember the title of her never-completed master's thesis in anthropology, something like "The Tent Determinant." For lack of a degree she never went into the field but instead took up charity work with the usual lost causes in between bringing up your mother.

But anyway, this domestic scheme, which I have elaborated in my *General Theory,* in the chapter entitled "The Adult

Guide to the Practice of Industrial Sex," will be disseminat-
ed throughout the world on the occasion of my "big one"
about seven years hence, under the auspices of the Thingie®
Foundation, which I have created for the promotion of my
ideas. One-hundredth of a cent from the purchase price of
every packet of Thingies® is now contributed to the
Foundation. When the endowment reaches a critical mass
within the upcoming five years, I will be able to count on my
ideas being as widely promoted as money can buy. The main
problem appears to be that my conservative colleagues to
the right become upset at anything more explicit than the
birds and the bees, and even that metaphor they suspect is a
liberal democrat reference to some so-called environmental
crisis.

And true, I do not practice what I preach. Or more
exactly, your grandmother and I do not practice what I
preach, yet our modus vivendi is not without interest. It is
summed up in the phrase and its variations, which you and
Rowena have already heard more than once: *I'm things, you're
people.* In theory this should solve everything, but unfortunately your grandmother expands and contracts the definition of both things and people to fit her personal needs and
agendas, to the point that what may appear to the naked
unbiased eye as a *thing* on day one, a house or a car, becomes
the next day a *person* enwrapped in a tangle of emotions and
memories and bizarre desires; and frequently vice versa. This
appears to be tied to her theory, or whatever, of *blossoming.*
As in, if I quote correctly, *Every person and even every object has
a special moment of blossoming, when it glows and becomes radiant*

and almost explodes. I can feel it pressing against me, telling me to stay still, watch, listen.

My response has always been, *And then what, it wilts and dies and turns to compost?* Whereupon she becomes evasive. *Maybe. Who knows?* And to my repeated question, *Does it happen more than once?*, she simply gives no answer.

Be that as it may, the exceedingly fat two-volume Commemorative Collector's Special Edition of the *Comprehensive Encyclopedia of All the World's Cars*, which I have presented to you and which is now safely installed out of your reach at the top of the bookshelf, is a fine example of a list of things, not a few of which you now own in model form. Even though you are still a little young to make out some of the longer words, it is never too early to fill your vision and imagination with the *things* of the world, leaving your little sister the simpler task of figuring out mere *people*.

15. 1:12 SCALE 1966 VOLVO P-122 SEDAN

NEXT WEEK, ROWENA, I WOULD LIKE YOU TO BE especially quiet and patient during my Founder's Report to the family on the occasion of the 25th anniversary of the incorporation of Thingie® Corporation International and not squirm or wiggle or suck your thumb, which you should have stopped doing about four years ago, or otherwise cause your father to jump up and start loudly cooing at you in the middle of the presentation. His disruptions have already caused me to lose considerable pleasure in this annual event, when I detail by means of flip charts and computerized slides the inexorable rise of Thingie® Corporation International into the financial stratosphere. My labors here as an entrepreneur have all been for the benefit of the immediate family, notably your grandmother Deirdre, your mother Deedums, your brother Fabian (whose expensive treatments for his public-event-hiccup-syndrome seem at last to be paying off), and by reluctant extension your father Chip. Your uncle Fabian and his wife Patricia have been invited as usual, but not, I have specifically requested, their ten-year-old twin sons. Nor several layers of progressively distant cousins on Deirdre's side who have got word of the event and who have been clamoring for years to be included. This—to try to remind you to remain still and quiet—is why I am adding this 1:12 scale 1966 Volvo P-122 Sedan, two tone red and white, to your collection early. I will explain the importance of this car to my life as a young entrepreneur in due course.

As I understand they have been teaching you reading in school for a year or so, I hope you will regard the occasion next week as an opportunity to improve your vocabulary, adding the terms *capital*, from which *capitalization, dividend, profit, stock-split, option, proprietary, lawsuit,* and *bankruptcy*, to suggest a good starter sampling. These words will help you understand the fascinating history of the founding of Thingie® Corporation International upon the ashes of KlampTite-MagicMastic. The only thing I really owed your grandmother Deirdre family's old empire was the formula for the soluble agent for my Thingie® invention obtained by informal means from a retired KlampTite-MagicMastic chemist, who creditably wished to shore up his retirement plan badly damaged by the manipulations that eventually led to bankruptcy. Of course you would not know this through the thousands of pages of court testimony in which your grandmother's Delahunt uncles attempted to revive the company, the very company they themselves had ruined, by wresting away from me the Thingie® patent, a case which was eventually dismissed. The attendant publicity introduced the Thingie® to the world without me having to spend a dime on advertising. By the end of the trial the worldwide recognition index for Thingies® exceeded Jesus Christ himself and was a close second to the prophet Mohammed.

About the two-tone red and white Volvo P-122 four-door sedan. During the two years of the Thingie® litigation, I was advised by my personal publicity trainer to adopt a low-profile lifestyle intended to suggest that your grandmother Deirdre and I were living a life of frugality and economy and were bringing up our only child, your mother Deedums, without the benefit of private schools or dancing or violin lessons, suffering as we were under the burden of a lawsuit of historic proportions. Or soon lawsuits, when a new one was added, The United States of America vs. Thingie® Corporation International, charging us with restraint of trade and with monopolizing the market for our little Thingies®. But how, my dear little Rowena, could we possibly be accused of—add this one to your vocabulary, while you're at it—*monopolizing* a market which simply didn't exist until I invented the Thingie®? The events of this dark period of our lives had such a strong effect on little Deedums that she resolved at an early age to become an attorney in order to defend helpless corporations against the depredations of inherently anti-business Big Government.

Needless to say we won that one too. But during those years we had to pretend that we were simple middle-class folks driving sagging used cars and living in a middle-class neighborhood on the edge of a slum in Dayton, in order to buff up the myth of the underdog of humble origins taking on the entire *liberal democrat* government and Deirdre's evil uncles who had looted enough of KlampTite-MagicMastic to still put up a good fight.

This is the story I retell during each of my anniversary reports so that the family will retain a clear memory of the amazing history of my success and wealth, in order to reduce, if not completely eliminate, the risk of apocryphal anecdotes eventually polluting the account and twisting its meaning around to serve the agendas of *liberal democrats.* Such as your father.

You have my permission, wee Rowena, or somewhat less wee, now that you are six, you have my permission to carry into our grand living room, where the furniture will be re-arranged for the occasion, my latest addition to your collection, and to hold it quietly in your lap throughout. You are turning into quite the little lady now, and there are indications that you will soon have the good straight but small Tuggs nose and the full Delahunt lips. Though I'm not sure there's much we will be able to do about your father's large knees and short legs.

If Fabian's public-event-hiccup-syndrome erupts, please ignore it. Giggling, you may not have noticed, only makes it far worse.

16. NICKEL-PLATED SCREW-ON CHRYSLER HUBCAP, C. 1929

I HAVE DECIDED, FABIAN MY BOY, TO OCCASIONALLY diverge from my original plan by presenting to you and your little sister exact replicas of separate and unique items from my own collection of automobilia, despite the possibility of complications which may arise from the fact that your two collections will no longer be identical, as I originally intended, in order to minimize if not completely eliminate questions of sibling rivalry. But these, I now fear, are likely to arise no matter what I do—given the genetic material you have unfortunately inherited from your litigating father. And what greater pleasure (for me) than to pass on while still in good health and spirits replicas of my little treasures which you would receive sooner or later upon my death, but without my lucid explanations of their origins and histories to accompany them. This will take place tomorrow on my return from Sydney. As ever I have a few hours to scribble a few words, on this night flight when it's too late on one continent and too early on another to conduct any useful business.

The Chrysler hubcap, circa 1929, is an exact replica

(including scratches and dents) of the first of more than three hundred hubcaps I acquired throughout my childhood neighborhood, usually on the way home from friends' houses on my bicycle just after dark, visiting the old cars and utility trailers made out of old cars' front axles parked in back yards. My anonymous exploits even attracted the attention of the newspapers, but only after I had amassed a collection too large to hide under my bed. Also my room had become redolent of axle grease—which I claimed I was using for one of my chemistry-set experiments. Now for those so-called biographers who have charged that I honed my famed entrepreneurial skills by filching my neighbors' hubcaps—or, even earlier, at age five, by managing to spirit little Arthur Byers's enormous collection of burnt-out Christmas tree bulbs in its entirety out of his house during his birthday party—I can only say that the real point is that I was able to recognize an opportunity when I saw one. And obviously, a good half of any opportunity is another's indifference or negligence. The editorials and letters to the editor about the "Jalopy Hubcap Thief" make for entertaining reading—especially given the extraordinary rise in value, from nothing, of my hubcap collection, for which we have just added on a special room to the Manor, next to the gallery housing my collection of antique light bulbs and neon light signs, including a corner dedicated to Arthur Byers's former collection of burnt out Christmas tree light bulbs. Some day I'll pull the clippings out of the vault and let you study them.

As I also said to your little sister, you may take this or any other item from your collection to my annual Thingie®

presentation to the family, as long as you promise to hold it carefully in your lap while I am speaking, in order to entertain yourself during those moments when my train of thought will undoubtedly outstrip your young understanding. I also expect it will help with your recent little hiccuping condition. There is hope, let me reassure you. After several false starts, your father again, with his unfortunate habit of applauding long after everyone else has stopped, with a sour and sarcastic expression on his face—after several false starts you have learned when and how to clap and have also learned to not clap in the middle of intense dinner-table conversations just to draw attention to yourself. You are to be congratulated for your new restraint.

I will be making several important announcements during my talk, to the effect that both profits and Thingie® share prices have reached dramatic new historic highs, adding two new billionaires to the family—namely you and your little sister, through various trust arrangements. Which makes you far wealthier than your father, but that's his problem, not yours. You may of course applaud at this news, though I would caution you against boasting of your future wealth to your kindergarten in part because your fellows will probably not fully understand. Worse, your teachers are likely to become resentful and sullen, particularly should they attempt any number of mathematical calculations that might serve to plumb the enormous gap between you and them. I don't know how to advise you to deal with your father, who has chosen not to participate in any of the family stock distributions, at least directly, even though of course he does via your mother, who does. In effect this has turned him into a relative pauper within the family. His own fault, of course.

You will notice that I no longer present directly my net worth as graphed by the minute throughout the day on the video projection system in my Manor bedroom and by a similar system on my 737, as I consider it indecent to examine it in public, though I am always pleasantly surprised to find myself rising on all those annual lists published in financial magazines—followed inevitably by sycophantic articles with titles like "How Billionaire Leon Tuggs Does It—We Think" but which are really crude gropings about for what they imagine to be my feet of clay. They look everywhere, they look into all the lawsuits, which are a normal cost of doing business, they pry into family tiffs with Deirdre's relations, and then, finding nothing, they purport to discover improper liaisons invented out of the whole cloth. Feet of clay? What they will discover, my little Fabian, when they rub off enough of the clay they themselves have splattered, what they will discover are toes of steel.

Old Chippo, your yacht-owning *liberal democrat* father, must be experiencing some interesting thoughts on the occasion of our local graffiti artist striking again for the fourth time last night, probably not long before my departure for Chicago and points west. Your mother has just phoned with the news. It turns out that we may have an educated vandal with an intellectual or philosophical bent at work, of radical leftist leanings, possibly some old Marxist from my former alma mater. Though the police are more inclined, I gather, to look among the vast servant class of the area who outnumber property owners two to one, and over half of whom are illegals.

This time the victim was the hull of your father's yacht drydocked over on the Sound, on which our artist spray-painted in red the following inscription half the length of the hull: SOCIALISM FOr THE rICH, FrEE ENTErPrISE FOr THE POOr, in letters tall enough to be visible from the I-95 northbound lanes at a distance of a quarter mile. Quite a feat, if I may say so myself. Unfortunately your father's ideology does not allow him to parse the statement to his advantage, to the effect that of course the rich who pay so much more of their income in taxes deserve proportionately more support in the form of those various government programs that seek to compensate them for their original sacrifice. You two are a little young yet to understand how or why the lifestyles of our major taxpayers—and mine may be taken as a prime example—are maintained and improved through educational and foundation endowments to the best schools, and transportation infrastructure improvements favoring those most able to appreciate them, plus corporate tax breaks and subsidies which keep the money flowing through the right class of citizens and their very carefully chosen representatives in government. And why, therefore, the poor must be left to fend for themselves until through hard work they have contributed enough to cover their keep, learning the ropes of capitalism at the most useful level in the process, which is to say learning to respect the value of money and indeed to accept it as our most effective god. Here, I must say, I part company with my colleagues to the *Neoconservative Christian Right* who attempt to hide the bounty of free-market capitalism beneath the billowing robes of Christ and the Apostles.

But I fear I have used this delay, a forced stopover in Salt Lake City while a front moves down past Seattle, to march a little beyond the range of your intellectual capacities and still-dormant political sensitivities—though by the time I bestow these words upon you, in the form of a handsome leather-bound volume to accompany your collections of model vehicles, I trust you will be upright and articulate defenders of the vast empire your grandfather has single-handedly assembled by leveraging garden-variety subsidies and tax breaks into the stratosphere, so to speak.

Where, the captain has just come back to tell me, we will be again in about twenty minutes. Or if not quite in the stratosphere, we'll be a good 30,000 feet above the teeming masses of minimum-wage earners.

I thought I would use this flight over the Atlantic again to record the resounding success of my annual show and the delight and surprise with which everyone—well, there is always an exception, of course—greeted the tripartite video projection screens which occupied the entire east wall of your grandmother's 4000-square-foot living room, the first time we have not used our 100-seat basement screening room, preferring a more intimate space. And everyone seemed enthralled—there's always that exception to the rule, however—by the new archival footage of the early days of Thingie® Corporation International, in film, video, and slides, as it gradually took over and modernized the old KlampTite-MagicMastic factories and office buildings. Equally stunning was the footage recording the acquisition and restoration of the historic estate of the Barbed Wire Robber Baron for our Michigan research center. It was that particular Delahunt of course who back in the nineteenth century laid the foundations for KlampTite-MagicMastic with his Barbed Wire Consolidated Corporation. This emerged, as you all know, from the strongest of the three units into which the Barbed Wire Trust was irresponsibly broken up by the federal courts in 1901. My collection of antique barbed wire and contemporary razor wire, possibly the world's most complete, will be housed in the new fifty-eight-room annex to the recently completed fifty-nine-room extension of the Manor.

Of course I realize there was probably an overwhelming amount of information in my three-hour presentation for children of your age, Fabian and Rowena, which is why I gave you score cards of my own design on which you could check off up to sixteen different old cars, all of which you should be familiar with from your collections and the encyclopedia, as they appeared in various film and video clips. I even made things easy for you by enhancing their images with almost imperceptible freeze-frame instants. But alas,

Rowena, you flunked entirely, while you, Fabian, checked only six on the list—it would seem before you went to sleep—though three of those were wrong. I gather those marks you made were checks. I will ask your mother whether she considers those long worm-like scrawls to be signs of intelligent life in that little brain of yours. But I do appreciate your controlling your hiccup condition until the final two minutes of my presentation.

But I don't think your squeals of delight, Rowena, helped at all when my high-powered surround-sound system shattered one of your grandmother's crystal vases and sent her rushing from the room in tears—though conveniently at a time when an intermission was called for.

It was an heirloom, she sobbed in the bedroom where I finally tracked her down. *Heirloom means there will never be another exactly like it.*

This of course is nonsense, I said. *A telephone call will make another one just like it, only better. Utter nonsense.*

You just don't understand.

How very true. I don't understand. I never have and never will. My lack of understanding has propelled me to the pinnacle of wealth and success—but no matter.

It was my Aunt Edee's, my favorite aunt.

You won't know the difference. This, it turned out, was an unwise return to the original proposition.

I will know the difference until the day I die.

I can hardly wait.

Cruel beast! she shrieked.

I'm going back out there to resume my show, I said after ten deep breaths. *Do you want to come out and secure the rest of your crystal, or shall I turn up the volume and blast it all to smithereens?*

Smash everything if you want, I don't care!

I returned to the living room and ordered Deedums to call the housekeeper to secure her mother's crystal either by removing it or by covering it with soft cloths, and I announced that the show would resume in exactly seven minutes and that if *anyone needed a quick nap now might be a good time,* as I could see that both of you seemed to be synchronizing your drooling onto the arms of your easy chairs and your eyes were looking up at the ceiling with a complete lack of focus. Ah, youth. Though you seemed to have reverted to an earlier pre-vertebrate phase of childhood by three or four years. Your father was scratching his crotch, sure sign that something was in the wind. (I was pleased to read the other day that he was finally cited for contempt of court for what he was apparently determined to make his trademark courtroom gesture.) But fortunately your grandmother pulled herself together enough to return to the living room, though she picked the armchair that was at the very end of the room, a good fifty feet away. I was surprised when you said, Rowena, *I want to sit with Grandma,* but equally gratified when your mother properly restrained you with a crisp, sharp command, and forcefully hissed into your ear: *You're going to sit right there young lady until your grandfather has completely finished, understand?*

Whereupon I resumed my triumphal survey of the rise of Thingie® Corporation International to its near-top position within the international corporate world. Images flashed on the screen of all the logos assembled through takeovers, mergers, and acquisitions, and the surround-sound raised the hairs on the back of my neck. Standing to one side, I waved my laser pointer like a conductor his baton, up to the climactic moment when Thingie® product identification conquers the world and virtually everyone from the jungles of New Guinea to the ice packs of Canada's Northern Territories knows what a Thingie® is and what it's used for. A brief financial summary of the corporation flashes on the screen against a background of fireworks bursting in air, and then, instead of *The End,* the words, *JUST THE BEGINNING.* Images then fade, music reaches a crescendo and then trails off into silence.

This was when your father jumped to his feet. You were snoring peacefully, Rowena—and you too, Fabian, until the violence of his words woke you up and your hiccups resumed.

I am not a shareholder, sir—that slimy curry-favor "sir" of his drives me up the wall—*but my wife, your daughter is, and so are my two children, whose father I am. As their father and therefore their moral and ethical custodian*—

Chip, Deedums hissed, *couldn't you just stop right now? Another time, perhaps!*

He gave a quick exasperated shrug at her interruption but then plunged right on in. *As their custodian, I would like to ask you, sir, just what Thingie® Corporation International intends to do about the environmental problems its products are creating all over the globe?*

What environmental problems? Thingies® create no environmental problems. *It's the environment that's the problem. It's been the problem since the Year One. Getting rid of your so-called environment has been the main purpose of the march of technological progress and the conversion of nature into useful manufactured objects like Thingies® and other items of our fantastic and widely diversified product line without which your law firm, for one, could no longer function in the modern world.*

This is my standard response to attacks by so-called environmentalists who merrily buzz on using the tools and fuels of the modern world just like everybody else—but then go and excuse themselves with an occasional frown and a chest-beating expression of guilt, such as your father was now attempting. I thought of course he knew better by now. But no.

Are you aware, sir, he blundered on, *that there is a glob of Thingies® all stuck together the size of a small iceberg floating off the coast of Southern California and that Thingies® have caused the deaths of millions of ocean-going fish by getting stuck in their gills and seabirds by getting caught in their throats, do you realize—*

Chip would have gone on and on of course had not you, Rowena, in a fit of anxiety pulled off the right rear wheel of the model Volvo P-122 and popped it in your mouth and then began making choking gestures. Fortunately your nimble mother grabbed you by the ankles and hoisted you as far aloft as she could and slapped your back, to the tune of you, Fabian, suddenly hiccup-free, chanting *I see England, I see France, I can see your underpants.* By now everyone was shouting, including your grandmother, who rushed the length of the room screaming *Call 911!*—until the little black wheel came dribbling out of your mouth encased in a gobbet of spit and rolled out onto the carpet, where I swooped it up and wiped it off and snapped it back on to the Volvo's rear axle, making it as good as new again.

With that, my annual show ended. I left everyone to soothe you, Rowena, with reassuring cooings and pettings and ticklings, while I sauntered out to the verandah to smoke a solitary cigar—one personally presented to me by Fidel, if I remember correctly—and contemplate the global reach of my endlessly profitable works, with your little jingle, Fabian, pleasingly echoing through my brain.

You might eventually be pleased to learn that I have entertained the captain and the entire crew with it on this Transatlantic flight—and of course I was quite delighted when the first rays of the sun illuminated the Channel and the intercom phone rang and I picked it up and the captain chanted, *I see England, I see France. . . . Right on schedule, sir*

Little Fabian, we have already had this conversation but I am nonetheless putting its substance in writing during a flight to Helsinki in order that you may look back on this experience from the perspective of future years and therefore extract more and more meaning from it with the passage of more and more time. I think I was successful in conveying to you my state of agitation when I looked up at your collection on the top two shelves of the bookcase opposite your bed and noticed that the 1:18 scale metallic blue 1954 Volkswagen Sunroof was clearly missing. You denied at first that you knew it was missing, odd since you must stare up at your collection every time you lie down in bed—well at least I hope you stare up at it—and with your exceedingly keen sense of sight you would have noticed any of the fourteen models and the encyclopedia being at even the slightest angle off from its habitual position. After all, did you not recently say to me, *Why is one of your ears bigger than the other, Grandpa?* You are expert in the fine distinctions, little Fabian, so don't try to pretend otherwise.

I do however have to admire your sophistry, in saying that it was not missing because it was now at Ricky Wong's house, in *his* room, on top of his *dresser*, presumably now part of *his* collection. Finally you admitted the truth, in the wee-est of voices.

I traded it, you said.

And for what did you trade it, Fabian? What? Louder, Fabian. Confess like a man.

Marbles, you whispered.

I demanded to see the marbles. You got out of bed and padded over to your closet in your dinosaur pajamas and dug them out of the dark corner where you had hid them and then dutifully brought them over and handed them to me, with a slightly proud look showing off your fine new Delahunt teeth, which sooner or later the rest of your face is bound to grow into, as if the marbles were great and valuable treasure. But, alas, they were ordinary clear glass marbles faintly tinted, a dime a dozen, a dime a gross, a dime a container load, in a frayed muslin sack.

Trading your birthright for a mess of potage, I suggested. *So it's come to that, Fabian.*

From then on, Fabian, you were no doubt so miserable that you missed the import of my little discussion of trading. I could tell from the way you tried to pull your lips over your teeth and rolled your eyes in panic. So I will repeat how you must realize that the goal of trading is not to exchange one object of value for another which you imagine will be of equal value, when you finally possess it. No doubt there are sayings floating around your little group of third graders to the effect of *Fair and fair alike* and ungrammatical variations of same, but these are all ruses, tricks if you wish, to conceal the basic fact that in the hands of the strong and cunning trading is a way to have your cake and eat it too. The sense of this apparently mysterious saying is right now being revealed to you. The long and the short of it, Fabian, is that the object of trading should be to end up not with the best marbles, hardly the case here, but with *all* the marbles *and* your 1954 Volkswagen Sunroof to boot. I had thought to wait until you were somewhat older before instructing you in these techniques but I see now I have waited too long.

Still there seemed to be nothing that could be done in the present situation except to point out that you have been screwed by Ricky Wong, who has bedazzled you with sparkling pieces of glass worth a tenth of a cent in order to pry from your grip a custom-painted scale model that could eventually fetch a price equal to the cost of the actual car bought new in 1954. None of the alternatives to reverse this transaction were savory. I did not see you having the spine, Fabian, to march over to Ricky Wong's house in Langston Farm Lake and Turf Estates and fling the sack of marbles down on his bed and aggressively demand your 1954 Volkswagen Sunroof right back, in an act of what we used to call, before the days of political correctness, *Indian giving.* Nor could I see you stealing into Ricky's bedroom and dropping the model into the knotted sleeve of your jacket and then deliberately tripping the Wongs' security alarm and wandering away in all the confusion as successive waves of security guards from Langston Farm Lake and Turf Estates and police down from Fairlawn-Fairview Lake Village roar in with sirens howling and lights flashing. As I might have done.

Under the circumstances, I had no choice but to personally intervene. The Wong money, you should have known as it would have saved you some grief, comes from commodity trading. You have to watch those people like a hawk.

Mrs. Wong, this is Leon Tuggs, Fabian Hoch's grandfather, I said on the phone, *I need regrettably to report that your delightful son Ricky engaged in a grossly unfair trade with my grandson Fabian, passing off to him a worthless sack of glass marbles in exchange for a priceless custom-made model of a 1954 Volkswagen Sunroof, a family*—but here I hesitated to utter the word "heirloom"—*part of a family collection I have been painstakingly assembling for my grandchildren. I wonder if you could send it back as soon as possible. We're all quite sick at heart about the misunderstanding.*

She dropped it by the next morning when I happened to be stopping by your house for a minute but she was probably so overwhelmed at meeting your famous grandfather— the covers of two national magazines this week—that she failed to ask for Ricky's marbles back.

I hope it isn't damaged in any way, she suggested with a little smile, pulling it unwrapped out of a leather shopping bag and handing it to me.

No, at first glance it looks just fine, Mrs.Wong, I said, flipping it over on its back. *Other than perhaps a bent axle. But just to be sure I'll go over it later with a magnifying glass.*

If there's any——

I silenced her with a seigniorial sweep of the hand and slowly shut your heavy paneled front door and made my way through your house to restore the 1954 Volkswagen Sunroof to its rightful place on the next to the top bookshelf in your bedroom.

Enjoy the marbles, little Fabian. I doubt Ricky Wong will ask for them back. If he does, tell him to call the Chicago office and ask my secretary to pass on the message.

So that's your little lesson for the day on how to turn a bad trade into a good one.

I believe I was explaining, my little Rowena, how your grandmother and I suffered horrendously by having to drive old well-used cars, such as the Volvo, when our tastes were so much better, and for that matter our real financial situation, which we had to conceal from the courts. Just so you won't think we always had it easy. Pretending to be poor is probably much worse than actually being poor because you are constantly surrounded by goods and opportunities which you know perfectly well you could just reach for and possess and enjoy without the slightest hesitation—if only circumstances would allow you to shed the disguises of poverty. For all I know the truly poor may have these very same thoughts but the difference is that while they know they will never be able to afford the tastes they have unfortunately acquired, we know that we can. Indeed, we will be able to afford any tastes we might end up acquiring. Yet given the KlampTite-MagicMastic spies, we had no choice.

This was the point at which your father barged into your room and swept you up out of your bed to congratulate you on your excellent grades at the end of first grade and report that as a very special present he had ordered a new French chateau-style dollhouse with real plumbing that actually worked for your backyard miniature subdivision. Had there been another adult present, he or she would have confirmed my suspicions that your father had forgotten that this was the big day of your first-grade graduation and had been reminded of it by Deedums while rushing through the house on those short legs of his, late home from work, to say goodnight to you. Be that as it may, he gave you a good-night kiss, or several kisses, while turning his bright hypocritical smile in my direction and speaking with deliberate rapidity, *I hope you're pointing out to her that these models you love to wax sentimental about are all made in sweatshops by teenage girls while the actual thing, the real cars, were made by union labor.*

Like every other object in the house? I suggested, standing up and slipping from the room. I refrained from pointing out that I could walk from room to room in your parents' seventy-two-room house and with a margin of error of perhaps three percent identify the countries of origin and manufacturing processes and associated labor costs of every single object within them and that by the end of the tour, on the basis of a few notes scribbled onto my own palm, I could give you a number (that later could be scientifically demonstrated to be accurate within the above margin of error) for any one of the five major fiscal indices, which include raw materials, transportation, fuel, taxes, and labor. Most likely the average labor cost in current dollars for every object in the house would be about twelve cents an hour. *Which, my dear Chip,* I easily could have said, *is why you with all your* liberal democrat *flimflam ideas is why you are rich and the rest of the world is poor. Do the math, as they say.* But I chose not to display my expertise on that particular occasion as I have on so many others, notably on national TV.

We had already said goodnight and even had I stayed longer I would have deferred to an older age our inevitable discussion about *unions*, my little Rowena, to a time when you will be more able to comprehend such matters. You are still too young to notice that your father, who loves to bask in his own sentimental *liberal democrat* fantasies, is not urging the housekeeper, the cook, your nanny, the two grounds-keepers, and his resident mechanic, to rush out and join the appropriate labor unions—which would probably cause him to be run out of Fairlawn-Fairview Lake Estates on a rail, tarred and feathered, which would be the first such incident in the neighborhood in three hundred years.

And I will eventually point out that it's a matter of pride to me that not one Thingie® in the world is or has ever been touched by a *union* hand or for that matter ever will be.

Thingie® Corporation International takes such good care of its employees that there is simply no need to add yet another layer of bureaucracy between the worker and his or her pay-check—and indeed Thingie® Corporation International has proven to be one of the favorite investments of *union pension funds* because of its predictable and spectacular rise in value. Someday you may be called on to defend the minimum wage. What I suggest you do on that occasion is to contemplate the purpose of your own allowance, which by then you will also understand. The real purpose of the minimum wage is to provide an allowance to the young and the poor during whatever period of time is required for them to attain that degree of financial maturity for which they will deserve something better. The minimum wage, more importantly, allows the faster accumulation of capital for the well-off, an invaluable incentive to the poor to struggle in an upwardly mobile direction and without which they would remain in an unambitious and lethargic state. It is the old stick and carrot arrangement, in short.

I know your little antennae are very sensitive—but you would be wrong to misread the regular altercations that your father and I experience as a sign that I do not like the man, am not fond or him, or feel less protective of him as a son-in-law than I do toward your mother, who is my daughter and only child. Of course I like the fellow—he is your father, after all—though of course I would like him far more if he would agree with my ideas, which are the reasoned and seasoned products of my long experience. Or if he could at least now and then pretend to agree with them rather than trying to *bait* me on every chance encounter or at every dinner party or special event or social occasion at which we both have the misfortune of being present. Before such encounters it is a common point of discussion between your grandmother and me exactly which door Chip will enter with knife raised ready to strike—a figure of speech here, nothing more—and whether this time he will perhaps go too far, forgetting that in doing so he may injure the precious little hostage, you my pet, that we hold in common. Or hostages, if we include your brother and your mother Deedums. Who, I would never say publicly, was the one who got us into this mess in the first place by marrying into a family of prominent *liberal democrats.*

17. 1:8 SCALE 1980 FORD FAIRMONT STATION WAGON

WHEN THE KLAMPTITE-MAGICMASTIC LEGAL TEAM abruptly withdrew its patent infringement suit and proposed an out-of-court settlement that would release all claims against my three key Thingie® patents, I settled for the sake of your grandmother and the benighted rustbelt Delahunts. Just before that felicitous event, I bought the bottle green 1980 Ford Fairmont Station Wagon for very little money, another back-of-the-lot special but one which, you now know, was to become my signature vehicle for the decade during which my net worth rocketed up through the six and seven and eight digits on the strength of the runaway success of the Thingie®. But rather than do what any fool would do in my newly flush position, which would be to buy the most expensive car I could afford, I decided to hang on to the old Ford as a symbol of the frugality and thrift with which I managed the whole of Thingie® Corporation International. I cannot now count the number of media pieces with titles like, "Worth Hundreds of Millions, Leon Tuggs Still Drives His Old Ford." *His Old Ford* of course modified with a supercharged V-8 instead of the original underpowered straight

six, tires two sizes larger and suspension and brakes bol-
stered accordingly, bullet-proof windows and armored panels eventually added, plus two types of satellite communica-
tion systems. I used this humble car for official appearances
and occasional ceremonial drives between the Chicago
townhouse and headquarters or between the Fairlawn-
Fairview Lake Manor and my private airport. It was always
left deliberately out in front of the house in the weather, to
help weather it, and to enable the paparazzi to take tele-
photo shots of it through the bars of the gatehouse gate a half
mile away.

You will note, Fabian and Rowena, that this is your
first 1:8 scale model, meaning that that one foot of the
model equals eight feet of the reality; hence its large size of
almost two feet long. I trust you will also note that they
finally got right the scale model of your very own grandfather, in his forties, behind the wheel, dressed in his work
shirt and Levis—what I call my signature media uniform,
used except for formal meeting with heads of state. I won't
go into the cost of this.

People like their billionaires to make occasional displays
of frugality—I make a point of picking up trash or ordering
my underlings to do so on my tours of facilities, even though
I know full well by now that the wadded up paper towel or
empty juice bottle has been placed along my route for the
photo opportunity the gesture provides. Usually I wave these
objects at the press with jocular comments on what a trashy
lot they are. Such details help bond the poor to the rich and
ease the reluctance which even the poorest may occasionally

feel as they contribute a penny here, a tenth of a cent there, to my vast personal wealth, even in the most obscure corners of the earth. There the passion for Thingies® rages unabated, particularly among those many primitive societies in which the Thingie® is considered an essential part of any wedding or funeral or shrine or grave marker and where even the poorest beggar child is expected to contribute at least one Thingie® to the communal display. Even my greatest detractors—yes, I have those too—have admitted that this is a triumph of marketing without historical precedent.

Much fuss is being made about all those billions of people who live on less than a dollar a day, but look at three hundred dollars a year not in terms of dollars but in terms of cents. Three hundred dollars equals 30,000 cents. Or even better, three hundred dollars equals 300,000 tenths of a cent. Given the crumbling of Third World economies, we have begun to consider reconfiguring our returns in terms of hundredths of a cent. Then three hundred dollars equals a staggering 3,000,000 hundredths of a cent. Now we're talking real money. If they only knew how rich they were in hundredths of a cent, I'm sure the poor would stop whining forthwith. As I have repeatedly explained to you, Fabian and Rowena, the fraction of a cent is where the real action lies in global capitalism.

So this 1:8 scale model, another pricey custom job, represents the subtle touch I have always had with the little people of the earth, a source of considerable pride. Treat the model accordingly, my pets.

* * *

You were eavesdropping yet again, I am certain, when I called the current President of the United States *the Big Penis* in a heated argument during our after-dinner brandy with your *liberal democrat* father, for which I have no need to apologize, having not said such a thing to either of you, directly to your innocent faces. If you persist in stealing out of your rooms and coming downstairs every time you hear voices rising in that echo chamber of a dining room your parents "designed especially"—to encourage acrimonious dinner-time debates, it would seem—then I fear you'll be getting exactly what you deserve.

However, I would do well to explain. Of course I did not mean that *he* has a penis larger than anyone else's. In any case, as you have probably already learned in your swimming lessons, Fabian, the comparative dimensions here are all trivial and are usually hidden anyway as a matter of custom and law, as should be the case.

And it wasn't exactly what I had intended to say, which your father immediately picked up on, feigning high incredulity. *You're calling your own President that? Who happens to be a friend?* I recall that he tipped back his chair and tossed back his head and let out a stage laugh that easily could have filled ten acres of your property and awakened neighbors across the lake to boot.

Then he brought his chair back to position with a mad

gleam in his eye. Deedums was leaning across the table with
an outstretched arm and a supplicating look but didn't have
the time to say as she usually did during such crises, *Chip,
don't, please.*

He shot out, *Then what do you call his predecessor?*

The Little Prick, I snapped back. Of course. In my position
you would have said exactly the same thing, I'm sure. It was
at precisely this instant, Rowena, that your sneeze was heard
just inside the hallway. It took me some weeks to reconstruct
the rest of the evening, after your grandmother Deirdre had
returned from New York and had begun making the rounds
to restore peace in the family. Apparently your father, after
another brandy or two or three, but despite the urgings of your
mother—who eventually left the house at approximately
two A.M. to spend the balance of the night in the guest room
of an old friend—your father, I say, chose to call the Secret
Service and report my words, or some variation on them, to
some young official on duty. Within a day or two, this led to a
visit to Fairlawn-Fairview Manor one fine spring morning by
a discreetly armed young government agent in a dark suit with
a sallow complexion. He had the gall to ask me in my own living room whether my intent was hostile in calling my friend
the President whatever I called him. And how many firearms
did I possess? I explained that I owned three hundred and
twelve antique and contemporary hunting rifles, shotguns, and
handguns, all registered, inspected, insured, and recently
appraised at $3.8 million. In a special new gallery just finished
next to the one housing my world-class collection of vintage
and contemporary water pistols. Would he like to have a tour?

I beg your pardon, Mr. Tuggs?

Eventually he apologized. Which led me to explain, in a merry moment, that I was attempting to explore the ramifications of an admittedly excessive metaphor, to use one of the few terms that has survived from my days as a *communist university liberal arts* student.

Sir? he inquired, puzzled.

Forget it, I suggested and then moved on to point out that your grandmother and I have contributed to the Republican Party to the fullest extent allowable by law and then some. I alluded to my brief service in the cabinet of one of the BC administrations.

Sir?

I tried to clarify. *A little joke. BC means Before Christ.*

He held his pen in mid air. He really needed help.

Meaning "a long time ago." Very briefly, I did not explain. It turned out I was particularly unsuited for public service.

He looked down at his notebook. *Oh.* By then he was blushing and his temples were glazed with perspiration. *I'm sorry, Mr. Tuggs. We're being run ragged at the moment.*

I said I understood perfectly. I escorted him to the door with my tongue clamped firmly between my teeth so as not to suggest that the member of the family who should really be investigated was your *liberal democrat* father, whose diatribes on the character of the President are the closest things to sedition I have ever heard. For your sakes, my little ones, I held my tongue and gave the agent's perspiring hand a firm patriotic shake, even as I wondered who to bill for the time wasted, which was causing a cascade of meeting cancellations and postponements all across the country, through time zones from east to west.

From one of the chaise longues on the front veranda, while I was dialing the office I watched the official black Ford Crown Victoria circle the chestnuts and head back down the winding drive through the mile of dense hardwoods that buffer us from the outside world in the form of the Fairlawn-Fairview gated communities I have developed around the lake. I cannot believe, I thought while my secretary transferred my call, that riding at high speed in a huge bulletproof Cadillac—however unfashionable the actual car—and escorted by motorcycle police and Secret Service agents in large Ford Excursions is not one of the great incentives to aspiring to be President of the most powerful nation in history. And that having your hand rest lightly on the buttons of the machine that can launch supersonic missiles all over the world cannot be one of the most exciting experiences in an entire life. At the very thought I could feel sparks shooting from my loins. Of course it could possibly cause one's penis to grow a little. Likewise, I cannot imagine that some *liberal democrat* fool who in a fluke of massive voter incompetence happened to find himself in that ultimate office and who happened to wake up one morning and say to his staff, *Oh, I think I'll pop over to the Old Executive Office Building on a solar-powered electric scooter, thank you,* I cannot imagine that he would not soon be picked off by some special services rooftop sharpshooter, knowing he was protecting the nation and its global assets from someone who would just as soon give it all away.

* * *

Fabian, I don't know that I responded in an entirely satisfactory way the other night to the remark you made while I was sitting on the edge of your bed pointing out some features of the custom-made Ford Fairmont Station Wagon. From out of nowhere you interrupted me.

There's a boy at school who has two.

I was momentarily confused. Two what? Custom made models of Ford Fairmont Station Wagons? *Two…?*

You pulled your lips down over your increasingly fine Delahunt teeth and rolled your eyes in confusion.

Two what? I repeated.

You know, you said, then blurted out, *two things.*

I thought long and hard before suggesting what I thought you might be hinting: *Penises?*

You nodded vigorously before throwing your head beneath your pillow, leaving me with a troubling thought, which has haunted me ever since, I must confess. That there will soon be a young man out there, eventually a fully grown man, equipped with *two*, able to enjoy everything twice as much as everyone else, including especially me—now that is an extremely disturbing vision. At the very least, I might have to revise certain passages in my *General Theory*. At the very most—but I nipped such thoughts in the bud.

From under the pillow I heard a noise, then giggles.

Speak clearly, Fabian, I commanded.

He charges, you said between giggles, *twenty dollars a look.*

Well, I thought, at least he's learning how to capitalize on his unusual feature. I'm sure he will go far.

With that I felt compelled to put the Ford Fairmont back in its place on an upper bookshelf and bid you good-night.

I left your room with troubling sparks shooting from my loins at the thought of somebody, anybody having not one but *two.*

Is there nothing sacred left in this world, I wondered as I shut the door.

18. 1:12 SCALE AERO COMMANDER

THE ACCELERATING SUCCESS OF THE THINGIE®— winner of the "American Product of the Year Gold Medal" for an unprecedented three years running—enabled me to reveal a secret passion for flying. (Fittingly I am jotting down these words on a night flight back from Beijing.) I obtained my pilot's license on my birthday, one of those big ones back then, and then took to flying from headquarters in Chicago to our various manufacturing plants and distribution centers, arriving minutes after a prop-driven transport plane had unloaded the 1980 Ford Fairmont Station Wagon above, so that I could then drive from the airport to my final destination. This was to become my routine through a succession of private planes and cars, all of which will be gradually added to your collections upon the usual special occasions, this one being Christmas.

This of course is my favorite time of year because Thingie® use increases so dramatically in the last ten days before Christmas, when every American simply has to have special holiday Thingies® not only all over the tree but under the tree as well, on the mantlepiece, and all up and down stairs and front walks, and even on the front grills of cars and trucks. Christmas of course is a wonderful expression of the true spirit of Christianity embracing the productive miracle of American capitalism, which delivers heaven on earth to all the worthy and faithful with approved credit ratings. The old saying, "A camel can pass through the eye of a needle sooner than a rich man can enter the kingdom of heaven," no longer applies in a world in which it is perfectly clear that American capitalism has brought the kingdom of heaven down to earth to benefit everyone who can afford the overhead, leaving all those camels and needles out there in the desert where they belong.

I should alert you, however, to another prize the Thingie® won, if only because you should be prepared should some classmate schooled in subversive *liberal democrat thinking* decide to become a young muckraker in order to curry favor with one of your closet *liberal democrat* teachers, despite my attempts through various endowments to keep the school curriculum within acceptable *Conservative Republican* parameters. The so-called "Rotten Egg Awards" are bestowed on or rather thrown at those "American industrial products contributing to the destruction of the health of the nation, the weakening of the social fabric, and the despoliation of the environment." I quote, reluctantly, from memory, leaving out more such claptrap refuted by the fact that the major victims of this award add up to a corporate product Who's Who of the nation's major export earners, to whose ranks I was proud to be added for many years running. But as I say, my little ones, you should know about this "award" now, coming from a friendly source within the family, so that the news will not be dumped on you by surprise by some envious fourth or fifth grader scheming to get an "A" at your expense. As a condition of my various contributions to the school's endowment, I have had the library meticulously cleansed of such material, and Internet access appropriately filtered, but these days you never know.

It is no secret that your father has prohibited you both from flying with me in any of my planes, large or small, but I trust he will not be so narrow-minded as to forbid you to sit in them when I finally finish the creation—only recently undertaken—of the Leon Tuggs Museum of His Personal Transportation with exact full-size real—not model—versions of the cars and other powered conveyances I have owned and driven and piloted over the course of my life. In a few cases we have been able to track down the original vehicles all the way across the country in California, such as the 1939 Ford Fordor, turned into a hot rod which we are dechopping and dechannelling and generally decustomizing. In a few other cases we have found suitable replacement vehicles needing few modifications to bring them back to their original condition. I have reason to believe that the Museum, which will be a life-sized mirror of the little collections that will eventually fill one wall of each of your rooms, will be the first of its kind. I would hope that both of you will see the Leon Tuggs Museum of His Personal Transportation as potentially the ultimate repository of your own collections.

While the matter is still fresh in my memory, Fabian, I

should add that I truly reveled in your third grade performance of the King in that delightful play, "The King and Queen
of Ice Cream," about a kingdom in which deserving children
spend their dreaming hours eating ice cream. Charming—
your painted-on curly black mustache and dramatic black
eyebrows, though they didn't quite go with your very blond
hair and blue eyes. I was particularly impressed by the way
you broke your wooden sword over the head of the "Diet
Spy" dressed in black—apparently preceded by some backstage altercation—which I gather was not in the script. You
certainly took care of that unpleasant character, and relieved
us of having to listen to more of his *liberal democrat* claptrap
throughout the rest of the play. I was, however, somewhat
confused by the end, in which you were all eating vegetables, while singing. Unfortunately my plane was waiting, and
I couldn't stay for the closing-night party, at which these
questions would have been answered.

A final note: The Aero Commander was also associated
with my acquisition of the last large tract of land in eastern
Connecticut on the edge of Fairlawn-Fairview Village, complete with a small lake, on the north side of which I
had Fairlawn-Fairview Lake Manor built. Opposite, several
smaller tracts were sold as sites for 10,000 square foot minimum houses, including your parents', the only other house
with good frontage on the lake, and a three-minute drive
from the Manor—enabling me to visit easily my lovely
grandchildren whenever I am at home. There were of course
the usual complaints at the zoning hearings about the "big
box" look of the Manor but my attorneys successfully

defended the design by pointing out my need for a sizeable climate-controlled space in which to house complete copies of English-language magazines, newspapers, court records, and books which either featured me or referred to me personally or to the development and evolution of the Thingie®. There you will find articles and advertisements and even footnotes, from scholarly works to supermarket tabloids dating from my very first mention in the press—the "Jalopy Hubcap Thief" article—to the present day. Also included are countless film and video clips and audio tapes of interviews and Congressional hearings at which I testified. At present, eight million separate pieces have been logged into the archives, which take up the entire north wing of the Manor, a complete tour of which you will be given at the appropriate time. I anticipate that this material about me will provide a lifetime—or two—of delightful reading and viewing for all of my heirs, including first of all you two.

Just as I was getting ready to wrap everything up, the captain called to tell me we have been re-routed to Frankfurt, owing to a strike threatened by, guess who, the French air traffic controllers union. I might as well take this opportunity, Fabian, to say how pleased I was that you came out to my new garage at the Manor all bright eyed to fetch me for dinner the night before last and actually evinced some curiosity about my budding collection of cars, one of which I had asked my mechanics to leave up on the hydraulic lift for the night so I could inspect its undercarriage.

As an engineer, being familiar with the underside of a car is often far more important than what you can see while standing and looking down into the hood compartment and other upper areas of a vehicle. Some of the happiest moments of my childhood were when I was able to lie in the dirt in the cool of the morning underneath the family Fords, identifying the components from schematic line drawings I found in a school library encyclopedia: axle, shock absorber, spring, frame, bushing, king pin, idle arm, oil pan, radiator drain cock, brake drum, and so on—words which I carried around in my memory like precious trinkets, rolling them between my thoughts until they became familiar with wear.

Unfortunately you quickly lost interest when I turned on the shop light and illuminated the various components in order to give you a lesson. You seemed to be only excited at the thought that the 5,000-pound Bentley Turbo—a model of which will be added to your collection at the appropriate time—might somehow come crashing down on our heads.

Can I make it go up and down, Grandpa? you finally asked.

I told you to press the red button to bring it down but failed to notice that one of my mechanics' rolling tool chests was just under the far rear bumper, which, as it lowered, came down on the corner and, before we could push the stop button, tipped it up on edge with a horrible screeching noise and then spun it across into the next bay into the side of the Mercedes 450 SL with a sickening thud and then a crash as the chest tipped over, spilling out hundreds of sockets and wrenches all over the concrete.

None of this was exactly your fault, Fabian, so this

time your trust fund will not be billed for the $17,000 esti-
mated to repair or replace the rear quarter panels of both
the Bentley and the Mercedes and the tool cabinet and to
realign the bent hydraulic lift.

And I'm sure everyone at the dinner table except me
was vastly entertained by your account of the mishap, which
you retold twice, bouncing up and down in your chair, while
your father struggled to be silent as a stone, fortunately, and
your mother interrupted only to suggest you not talk and
chew your food at the same time—until she had to lead you
away to deal with an onset of those hiccups of yours.

In researching various ways I might prepare you as my
grandchildren for inheriting the enormous wealth your
grandmother and I will leave behind for you first, and which
your parents will leave behind second, assuming our mortal-
ities will proceed in an orderly manner, I have yet to come
up with a foolproof method for you to enjoy what will soon
be yours unfettered by the ideas and schemes and judgments
of all those others—most of the world, in fact—who will
want to tell you what to do and above all what not to do with
your money. Perhaps on this flight to Hong Kong, I can best
begin by simply cataloguing all those types of people so that
you will more readily recognize them and thus spare yourselves from being led down the same garden paths again and
again.

By way of a preface, some thoughts about what money
is and why it was invented in the first place. Which is more

easily stated than explained—why mere numbers, mere pieces of paper, mere magnetic impulses can dictate the course of lives all over the globe. For the most part invisible and unknowable, money is in effect the most successful and longest lasting and longest surviving *god* that humankind has ever created, as can be seen from the fact that those who fail to properly worship money, for whatever reason, easily fall into a graceless state known as poverty. However, the *god of money* is not pleased to be worshipped openly, preferring to hide behind steel doors, in piggybanks, in wallets and purses, and generally out of sight. It is, in short, one of those gods who prefer to manipulate the world out of the public eye— like most of us in fact.

That explained, we can move on to how different types of people relate to the *god of money*—and particularly to the wealthy, who may be seen as the *high priests of money*.

First, there are the rare, and perhaps even mythical, persons who claim that money is of no importance at all, which is usually a clever disguise consisting of various public gestures feigning indifference to the transactions going on around them at all times, and pretending that paying for a dinner, or a newspaper, or leaving a tip were things that only the birds and bees do. Beware of these people, the money atheists, who do their scheming at night, in private. Your Ricky Wong, dear Fabian, may be one of these. This is typical of people who come from commodities-trading money.

Your new friend Christopher Burr may be among the class of hangers-on and sycophants and opportunists waiting with stone-like patience for crumbs to drop, as well as your

little gimme-gimme friend Harmony Solotov, who has managed to walk away with some of your best dolls, Rowena,
though happily nothing from your model car collection.
These people—the Solotovs—are into commercial real
estate. You always have to watch out for that type.

Then there are the outright schemers and swindlers
who regard you as a bank to hold up—I lump blackmailers,
muckraking journalists, and paparazzi here. These are the
temple ransackers and tomb robbers of old. All lawyers,
especially of your father's stripe, belong in this class—
though not of course your mother. And all doctors.
Excepting my personal lawyers and doctors. Though I sometimes wonder.

Then there's a whole class of people who will want to
feed off of you through commissions and tips and fees for various services, and who have developed a fine sense of what
the traffic can bear. They start out early, these ones, but at
least they know where the line needs to be drawn and usually won't overstep it for a while. They should pass a law requiring these people have their percentages tattooed on their
foreheads.

The most trustworthy people, up to a point, and providing they are not feigning innocence, of course—the most
trustworthy are those odd innocents from another planet,
who are also the most pleasant. You might call them the *money
agnostics*. I used to encounter them rarely and almost exclu-
sively on those occasional transcontinental flights when I
decided it was necessary to mingle with the hoi polloi once
again—in the old days before my own personal 737 when I

flew only coach, and only in seat 18A. Now and then I would have the good luck to be next to a seat mate who remarkably had no idea who I was.

But such innocents, when the scales finally fall from their eyes, are quickly all over you with the sort of importunate questions even the most hardened journalist will have reluctance in articulating, and will soon reveal themselves to be in one of the three categories above, if not all three at once.

This, my dear little ones, is the terrible world into which you must be prepared in advance to grow up, but thankfully not without having access to an endless fountain of good advice and sound experience, in the form of your devoted grandfather, more of which I will prepare in due course and distribute to you later at the appropriate moments of your coming of age.

19. 1:12 SCALE 1985 MERCEDES-BENZ 500SEL 4-DOOR SEDAN

I WAS ALMOST PREVENTED FROM BESTOWING ON YOU two this 1:12 scale model 1985 Mercedes-Benz 500SEL 4-door sedan, the first outward display of my growing success that I allowed myself to flaunt upon my annual income exceeding the one-billion dollar mark, on the occasion of your parents ninth wedding anniversary. One of those periodic eruptions of family discord with which we must now and then test ourselves almost made me postpone the presentation of this latest model, complete with scale models of your grandmother and me in the front seat and you two in the back seat—even though you two were not yet born in 1985. No matter that I have privately thought that your parents' wedding anniversary should be marked by a chorus of wailing women dressed in black and by men in dark suits bravely suppressing sobs. But I have always been willing to enter into the spirit of an occasion, whatever my personal feelings and beliefs, as I was concerning this one, however odd is the grandly public manner with which they usually choose to celebrate it. Unfortunately my shoelace happened to come untied just down the hall from their bedroom door, while I was on the way to your bedroom, Fabian, and I was forced to stoop to retie it and could not help over-hearing the following altercation. Somewhat unaware I had switched on the video camera sound—as usual, I had the machine along to record my presentation of the models to you two—and so accidentally obtained a muffled recording.

You know perfectly well, your father was whining, *that he simply hates parties organized by others for purposes not centered around him.*

Then give him a central role, Deedums courageously sug-gested. *I am his daughter, after all. He is central. Without him*—

Why not just give him a hunting rifle and let him shoot me in the middle of the party. That would be very central—

But one of them decided to slam shut the bedroom door and I was left to imagine the rest, which in fact I chose not to, appalled as I was by your father's violent imagination. Although on recollection the idea was not without merit.

But I was also left to my own devices, because as the afternoon and evening gathered steam—three hundred invited guests, probably fifty uninvited, various lambs and pigs being barbecued out back by the Panamanian Army, children splashing in the two swimming pools, *liberal democ-rat* teenage cousins and friends and criminal-element inter-lopers trying out drugs and sex in the upstairs bedrooms and bathrooms—it was clear that they, or Chip, your father, had "planned" the afternoon and evening without any kind of formal moment of observance during which they could be toasted as a successful, happily married couple—or toasted as the carefully groomed illusion of such—and I was threatened with being deprived of what I so excel at: the extended toast. Desperate at being outwitted, I paced through house and garden with my two bodyguards in tow, tearing myself away from countless attempts to ply me with investment advice, and probably downed too many scotch and sodas in my perambulations—until at last I found myself in front of the fireplace with a glass of champagne in my upraised hand just at that moment when my eye caught Deedums and Chip about to slip out of opposite French doors of the living room. *I would like to propose a toast*, I bellowed, handing my video camera to some young fellow standing next to me— who I mistook for one of my bodyguards owing to his dark suit. *Film this,* I said in a low voice.

I could not help but notice an instant of nervous silence, a quick little pall that fell over the room, suggesting that their little bedroom conversation I had overheard had spread out to become a regional if not national controversy. I was faced with a split-second decision: either I could gush hypocritically sentimental for perhaps thirty seconds, not my wont, or I could wax passionate about the state of the world for half an hour. In an instant of inspiration, I chose to do both. Though I must admit that in that very same crowded moment of insight there flashed a vision of my swiveling around and reaching up and pulling down the buffalo gun that Deirdre's great grandfather, the Delahunt who was the Barbed Wire Robber Baron, had once used to help make the West safe for cattle. I imagined raising it and pointing it across the room and discharging it into the chest of my daughter's *liberal democrat* husband. But instead I inflated my lungs and spoke.

After carrying on about what *wonderful parents* they were to my grandchildren, cloaking the caveats under a thick blanket of generalization, I launched into my memorized remarks about recent attacks by so-called *environmentalists* on the Thingie® itself and the innumerable manufacturing and labor practices of which they disapprove—even as their own offices and homes are plastered with the now indispensable product, citing down to the exact penny the amount a certain *prominent left-wing law firm* has spent so far this year on Thingies® and Thingie® products, without mentioning by name your father's firm. By now the initial flux of people rushing in and out of the open French doors had stabilized and there was a steady increase in the number of people crowding inside, holding drinks and plates of barbecued meat, and briefly whispering to neighbors, no doubt finding out what this was all about.

This was the moment I was hoping for and had prepared for, to announce my grand theory of cosmic recycling, in which I propose that what *environmentalists* suffer from is myopic tunnel vision with no sense at all for the long view, the very long view, the fifty- or one hundred-million-year long view. *Ultimately everything, even those substances deemed toxic by the Chicken-Littles of the world, will be smoothly and thoroughly recycled by one of the grand actions of the solar system or the galaxy or the whole universe itself. Everything, not just some things, will be frozen or vaporized or crushed back into the elemental matter, out of which we will be free to evolve again, from a clean slate. All attempts therefore to forestall the process by misguided efforts at so-called conservation are in themselves pointless and therefore wasteful and a drag on the economy through the lowering of profits of the corporate citizens of the world, thanks to which you are all here today.*

The elaboration of this grand topic took nearly half an hour, a constant race against the restlessness of the drunken crowd, during which dusk usefully turned to night—and I knew I should begin moderating my vigorous arm gestures so that when the moment came for your grandmother to approach me and touch my elbow, signal that I should begin to wind up, I should not accidentally strike her with an out-flung arm. The applause was not what I had hoped for, thunderous certainly, but coming just as I was filling my lungs for my usually inimitable last line. But perhaps as well. In the heat of the crowded room, perhaps an effect of the scotch, I realized that my crowning phrase, my last words, had vanished from my brain.

Here's your camera, the young man said, thrusting it back at me with a rather rough gesture. It was only then that I realized he was not my bodyguard after all.

20. 1:12 SCALE 1986 MERCEDES-BENZ 480SL COUPE

I HAVE COMMUNICATED TO THE CEO OF THE HOLLY-wood studio that Thingie® Corporation International has just acquired my displeasure with the fact that so often in a movie the villain drives the best cars, such as Mercedes-Benzes, BMWs, Rolls-Royces, Bentleys, and Lamborghinis—while the impecunious heroes, who live in ungated communities, invariably get around in old Fords and Chevys or even antique VW Bugs. Why, I ask, is reality being so clearly distorted here—reality which any reasonable person can observe by driving through all kinds of neighborhoods in almost any large city in America. What you will see is that the older and shabbier the car the greater likelihood of its being driven around by a member of the criminal class, and worse, that it is likely to be piloted in the manner of a battering ram, to judge from the sad state of its body work, or what is left of it. Here, my good children, are your villains, not the upstanding and hardworking *Conservative Republicans* who are paying taxes through the nose to keep these people on welfare and food stamps and trying to shore up their crumbling schools and neighborhoods and offering them careers in the armed forces and who, to dull the edge of their own selfless sacrificial pain as taxpayers, now and then go out and buy a fine brand-new expensive car.

I have had my personal digitizer go over the tapes of a couple of recent thrillers, *The Blackington Receipt* and *Stall*, and re-edit them to switch cars around so that the so-called heroes now properly buy the best money can buy while the villains get the rustbucket wrecks. This does create a jarring note, I admit, where the so-called heroes slip in and out of their fine motorcars dressed in ragged, dirty clothes, while the well-tailored villains appear quite at ease in their cars with ripped upholstery and dirty, cracked glass. However, at your ages, you may not notice. My personal digitizer is still working on this.

I have also conveyed my displeasure to the studio at the common practice of having the young athletic actor succeed at pinning the guilt invariably on the *old man* at the pinnacle of the latter's professional or business career, the *great mentor* or *senior executive* or *successful entrepreneur* who is found to be at the root of a conspiracy to murder usually an innocent young female who stands in the way of his obtaining one last triumph and ending his career in the blaze of glory of a long well-articulated speech and a dozen golden parachutes wafting down from the sky. It seems to me that most of these plots could be easily re-jiggered to turn the young athletic actor—commonly a closet *liberal democrat*— or even the seemingly innocent female, into the villain and convert the *old man* with his nice Mercedes or Bentley into the *hero* who saves the day, as is so much more common in everyday life. That way neither cars nor wardrobes would need to be altered. Expunging a few words would probably do it.

And perhaps adding a few lines about the strengths of the free market economy and how many of the shots inside cars and offices and homes in particular could be enlivened by the addition of whatever number of Thingies® might be necessary to reflect the realities of our times. Hundreds per scene, I would think. We have calculated that on average the office worker and car driver and a domestic partner at work in a typical kitchen either touches or looks at or otherwise interacts with a Thingie® every nineteen seconds during his waking life and that Thingies® figure in twenty-one percent of all dreams and nightmares.

All of this is consistent with the fact that the main purpose of Hollywood movies, as you two already know, is to teach people how to use and experiment with exciting new technologies—and how to recycle products of obsolete technologies by turning them into weapons or objects to be disposed of by blowing them up or pushing them over cliffs or sending them to the bottom of the sea.

You are too young to know that Hollywood taught America first how to drive and later how to use computers. On the same principle we're planning to teach America how to use the new Thingie® 2.0 on its forthcoming introduction, after three years of intensive research costing hundreds of millions of dollars. We have only recently leaked its final trade name, Thingamajig®, was well the name of the new luxury line intended for use in CEO offices and suites of select luxury hotels worldwide, the Thingamabob®, though its release date will be about two months after the Thingamajig®. Revenues are projected to rise twenty-three per annum ad infinitum, to the perpetual benefit of your inheritances.

In the course of placing the silver 1986 Mercedes-Benz 480SL Convertible Coupe with me in my motoring cap behind the wheel, also 1:12 scale, in its place on the next to the top shelf of your book case, Fabian—you were using the bathroom before being tucked in—my hand brushed against some folded up papers which, given this unusual location for them, I could not help but take down and briefly examine before stuffing them inside my sports coat. To my consternation and bemusement. I'm sure, Fabian, you know exactly what I am talking about, though by the time you read this you may have entirely forgotten the balloon-like figures in pencil with stick arms and legs and grotesquely enlarged items we used to call in the old days "private parts." I suspect this is not your work. A certain boldness of line suggests an older child, possible your cousin Barton Delahunt, who seems to specialize in coming into your room to test the strength of each of your toys and the various parts of your games, which often enough is not equal to his own. A tall heavy-set kid fed too much protein and with cheeks flushed with feverish visions of what he can crush or dismember, he is the only one of your playmates easily able to reach the top bookshelf by standing on a chair. The fact that he has not yet molested any of the models of your collection is testimony to the fear in which he holds me owing to regular threats I hiss to him in the hallway, to the effect that I will drown him in the toilet if he so much as lays a single finger on any one of the models in either your collection or that of your sister Rowena. I am mainly upset that he is the son of the most upright *Conservative Republican* branch of your grandmother's family (ConTain RazorWire, a long dormant but now successful branch of the Barbed Wire Robber Baron fortune, through some lucrative prison contracts—their personal worth being a modest $163 million), and has so stubbornly resisted the example and teachings of his parents.

I see he has also provided you with a catchy little verse to while away the dark hours of the night. *Mary had a little lamb and kept it in a bucket, and every time she went away the rooster used to fuck it.* I admit that it is very difficult to get these things out of the head once they are so insidiously inserted there, and I know it is almost impossible to resist the temptation to whisper them into the tender little ears of your playmates and even your little sister and watch the verse make the rounds of your third-grade class until finally they reach the leathery sunburned ears of your teacher Ms. Plummets (on whose account I have been stalling on my current annual contribution; the denseness of the school director, who seems oblivious to my many hints, is staggering) whose lifestyle and pedagogy leave much to be desired. From what I can gather she has banned chewing gum and Thingies® from her classroom, and from the garbled accounts you now and then provide, Fabian, she is trying to instill a sense of *guilt* in her students regarding their privileged backgrounds. I cannot convey to you the degree of anguish suffered by your mother—she wisely has concealed this from you—when you came home apparently proud, at least for a few minutes, that Ms. Plummets had enrolled each of her twelve students in a different *environmental organization.* Yours was a deliberate slap in my face, you could not entirely realize, being the *Pacific Northwest Tall Timber Alliance,* which has managed to put out of bounds to our paper-producing subsidiaries so many millions of acres that we have been forced to move our operations abroad, seriously degrading our profit margins in the process. When Deirdre called me in the middle of the night—I was over New Guinea—I got on the phone immediately to the Attorney General, demanding that he bring down the entire Bill of Rights on Ms. Plummets's shaved head and nose ring, but when it turned out she had bought these memberships out of her own salary and not out of school funds, we had to turn back the FBI just as they were preparing to cordon off the entire school.

But I stray. Given Ms. Plummets's *anarchist ideology,* once she finally gets wind of *Mary had a little lamb,* I will not put it past her to have one of you write it up on the blackboard so that—*this is typical liberal democrat thinking*—you can all memorize it and even chant it together and write term papers on it and organize a parade with banners and songs based on the lines, up and down the streets and docks of Fairlawn-Fairview Lake Village, to demonstrate how liberated she is.

I realize I have left too late in your lives my lectures on Industrial Sex—but also must add that your father has categorically forbidden me to address the issue with either of you—so it is likely that these words will reach you after all the damage is done, when you come of legal age and I can communicate with you freely and I no longer have to fear your father carrying out threats to seek a court injunction against me. All I need point out, however, is that your house, like any in the industrial world, is equipped with countless connecting devices which suggest that the screw or bolt fits into the nut, the plug into the socket, and so on, and that as a result there is no need to seek titillation in crude pencil drawings and obscene doggerels. There is quite enough just lying around.

Despite my urges to the contrary—a lit match would do it easily—I have decided to include Barton Delahunt's *art work* and *poetry* as part of the duplicate collection I am maintaining for you, along with copies of my videos of you and Rowena accepting each of the models and my late-night written ruminations on the subject, most of them composed in the air while the world sleeps below—as I am one of those fortunate mortals who is quite happy with three hours sleep each night. At any rate these duplications are insurance against the theft or destruction of your own primary collection, so that when you finally reach an age equal to my own and come across it you will be able to experience both the shame you should have experienced at your young age but also—to be frank and man-to-man about it—possibly a tickle of delight at the memory of the smutty little verse.

21. 1:18 SCALE 1988 LEARJET TWIN

T HE 1988 LEARJET TWIN WAS A CONSIDERABLE improvement in terms of speed and general capaciousness over what it replaced, the Aero Commander, which was necessary for me to keep up with our rapidly expanding business—though I was to continue to use seat 18A in commercial flights abroad for another three years. Much of the last part of the decade and through much of the ninetics I was constantly in the air giving talks, shaking up new acquisitions, opening new distribution centers and the like. As a result I was lucky to spend two or three nights a week at home in the Manor and often Deirdre was gone during at least one of them, away on her charity work for the usual lost causes.

Be that as it may, if you flick the switch on the underside of the Learjet fuselage it will turn on the battery-powered light inside, illuminating an excellent scale model of me sitting in a padded, swivel armchair, with my seat belt on, and a telephone receiver pressed to my right ear, in front of my flight desk. Your grandmother Deirdre, I regret to report, was hardly an enthusiastic partner in the explosive growth of Thingie® Corporation International. *Why do you keep wanting more?* she nagged me repeatedly, especially during our late night phone calls when I was in the air. *Why do things have to keep getting more and more complicated? A little grass hut on a deserted island somewhere, that is all I long for.* I had stopped bothering to point out that we already had several of those reserved for our exclusive use on our development at Tiki-Tango Atoll, but she was never satisfied. *With servants hiding in the bushes*, she quickly objected, *waiting to rush out with cold drinks or hot towels or ringing telephones?* Failing to understand as usual that if you don't employ the natives they'll resume their former lives of raping and pillaging.

I cannot count the times I have explained to her the difference between men and women, which I will pass on to you two young ones now in order to save you the trouble of trying to discover it later all on your own, with the usual disastrous results—except in the Tuggs family, which has been divorce-free for more than 150 years. And will stay that way.

Men, you see, love complexity in things but prefer simplicity in people, while women prefer simplicity in things but love complexity in people. This also accounts for the difference between manly *Conservative Republicans* and effeminate *liberal democrats*.

Things, my little ones: we live in the great crowning age of things, in which each year our national industrial genius picks up some hitherto simple object and makes it far better and more complex. The piece of chalk broken off from a cliff becomes the pencil cut from the forest and mined from the earth, in turn becoming the typewriter requiring iron mines and steel mills, in turn becoming the laptop, whose bits and pieces are drawn from the ends of the earth and which contain enough brainpower to launch a rocket to the moon and beyond. The wheel becomes the cart, becomes the bicycle, becomes finally the automobile with thousands of moving parts and electronic circuits, busying the restless mind of mankind through wakefulness and sleep. We have reached, my pets, an age of unimaginable complexity, a world of men making things and fixing them and throwing them away and making them over and over again, more and more complex each time, luxuriating in the intricacy they have mastered, destroying with one hand, building with another, faster, higher, wider, deeper, heavier, lighter. Men race to invent and make more and more things each year to see who can sell the most things, who can cover the entire earth with them and who can finally replace the so called natural world with man-made things—leading to that climactic moment when finally we, with all our things, become the natural world itself.

This should be not far off, according to the figures I am being supplied concerning the paving over of raw land and the converting of forests into useful industrial products like Thingies® and the plans for processing useless icebergs into drinking water and—of course—into bags of ice to help counter the effects of global warming, which I have always regarded as yet another business opportunity, perhaps the greatest ever in the history of civilization. At the present moment, the main tool is the computer—which appears to work flawlessly, however, only in the movies. I have talked to our studio about this and have suggested that computers ought to crash much more often in thrillers, which would add excitement to boring and predictable chase sequences.

Now I am fully aware that my philosophy of the complex has now and then been ridiculed by those critics who rightly observe that the Thingie® is paradoxically one of the most elegantly simple inventions of all time—while overlooking the fact that the Thingie®, unchallenged tool used to keep track of the proliferating things of the world, has been the foundation for the extraordinary growth in both the complexity and the sheer number of man-made things in the world. My private motto has always been *More things, more Thingies®*. And more Thingies® means more toys, more models, more shares, more bonds, more real estate for my own lovely two grandchildren.

To her credit, your grandmother at least understands this, the final outcome, though not the intervening processes in which mountains are moved and whole forests are pulped in order to provide her two little darlings with new bedding and new pajamas every month. As for everything else, I throw up my hands in despair. Deirdre simply does not understand that in a world in which things are accorded their proper respect, people will be forced to simplify their innate complexity and focus much more steadily on the needs and demands of their things and machines, a useful discipline and therefore a force for public good. It is for excellent reasons that mankind has begun to achieve a world in which more and more messy, complex people are attached to this or that machine and required to behave accordingly by punching buttons, moving mice, pushing pedals and levers, turning wheels, and switching on and off switches of various kinds. You may now and then see on TV crowds of people rampaging through streets and overturning cars and smashing windows, for which there is a simple explanation: these are people who have failed to find a machine to bond with and who are therefore expressing their resentment against all of the rest of us who have.

Complexity, in short, is a bonding mechanism, my pets, which you need to remember every time something goes wrong with a toy of yours or—later on in your lives—a tool or a complicated piece of equipment or machinery. We engineers are trained to make things as complicated and inscrutable as possible, which are clever and useful ploys to make people pay attention to their things and therefore bond to them—and also to bond in advance to the upcoming generations of even more complex things.

A last thought here will have to wait. In exactly two minutes a call will be coming over the red phone from the President. He's been very chatty of late.

22. 0-GAUGE 1928 PULLMAN PRIVATE OBSERVATION CAR

THE PURCHASE OF THIS PRIVATE RAILWAY CAR WAS the most stressful addition ever to my personal rolling stock in part because I realized far too late that I had been sucked into—at some investment consortium board meeting—a little rivalry game among several of my fellow entrepreneurs who had all recently out-vied themselves by snapping up a number of antique private railway cars that had come on the market. Never encouraged by my father in the first place, my interest in rail transportation ended definitively at the age of seven when I assembled my second-hand Lionel electric train set on a piece of cardboard on the upper bunk of my bunk bed. Everything connected, I ran the engine and tender and a boxcar and a flatcar and a tank car and a caboose around and around its circle until I threw the switch that sent the train down a dead-end spur and over the edge of the mattress, at the precise moment when Bobby Finn, who had spent the night in the lower bunk, stuck his head out. He required seven stitches in his scalp and I renounced all interest in rail transportation for many decades.

This O-gauge model that I am adding to your collections, Fabian and Rowena, on the occasion of your eighth
birthday, Rowena, was custom-made from the ground up by
a specialty firm, who gave only a slight discount for my
ordering four instead of one. That's me waving from the
observation deck—which, given the smallness of the scale,
is not entirely clear. My experience with the actual private
rail car was never satisfactory. Twice I was stranded on sid-
ings in the middle of Ohio, owing either to mechanical
problems in the trains my private car was attached to or the
tracks that it was on, and I was forced to summon a company helicopter to rescue me. Anyone can understand that
someone with my annual income from all sources, which
amounts to more than $300,000 an hour per eight-hour day,
cannot simply afford to sit around for several hours twid-
dling their thumbs while some *union* crew up the tracks
holds seminars on how to attach a nut to a bolt. Not that I
only work eight hours a day. Eighteen is more like it, not
counting flying time, such as right now, passing over the
lights of Vancouver-Seattle at 2:00 A.M.

A mistake, a mistake, but there you have it. I have just
watched the video of you two accepting your Pullman
Private Observation Cars and I can't say I blame you for
your lack of enthusiasm expressed by somewhat sour looks.
But where's the engine? you wanted to know, Fabian. I was
interested to note that neither of you thanked me this time
for the gifts; nor did your mother Deedums bother to
prompt you. The malign influence of your father, no doubt,
who has not said *thank you* in my presence for the last

decade. *Neat, cool, hey, nice, rich,* yes, but never *thank you.*

Be that as it may, the events surrounding the wretched private railcar stimulated me to bring my theory on the uses of mobility at last to fruition, both in practice and as a published volume. This coincided nicely with the somewhat unexpected runaway success of the Thingamabob®—which in fact robbed sales from the mid-line Thingamajig®, finally dropped only two years after its introduction—a success that enabled me to begin investing heavily in food-service paper goods and finally directly in food service itself, setting the groundwork for some radical fast-food improvements at a time when the great era of innovation was generally considered to be over.

Originally intended to be a privately-printed companion to my earlier tome on Industrial Sex, my new book, *A General Theory of Mobility*, was put in the hands of nine ghostwriters and shaped in record time into a long-term bestseller, helped by the fact that I suggested that I would be very pleased if every last one of my tens of thousands of loyal employees would buy a copy at the full retail hardback textbook price by means of painless electronic paycheck deductions. There are of course other inventive ways to make best-sellerdom happen, though that was the most profitable. Be that as it may, my theory states that in essence consumption of fuels and energy in general, in addition to food and non-durable goods, is an accelerating function of mobility as measured by speed. In other words, that is in words you two will soon understand but are probably not there yet, the more you move around and the faster you move around the more gasoline you or your parents will buy and use up and the more food, particularly fast food, and all the packaging attached thereto, you will consume, and the more likely you are to acquire other goods, perishable and even occasionally even durable, so-called, like new cars and pickups and SUVs. The Thingie® is one of those simple devices which lubricates and facilitates mobility, and of course the more mobile you become, the more Thingies® and Thingamabobs® you run through.

It follows then that, from the point of view of the enlightened entrepreneur, such as your grandfather, the more we get people to move around, to the point of having them constantly mobile, or almost constantly mobile, then the higher our profits will be and the higher the value of our shares and related investments will rise, and ultimately the greater will be your inheritances, my little ones. Human beings, however, even though they are increasing their tolerance for non-stop mobility, still apparently need to come to rest now and then. This is where television has proven so handy, in the way it continues the sensation of mobility by other means. My *General Theory of Mobility* posits that within the near future the experience of actual mobility and the experience of watching TV will ultimately merge and become indistinguishable; in other words, people won't know (or care) whether they are driving around or watching TV. I call it taking the "wind" out of the windscreen.

Our involvement in food-service paper goods led to a revolutionary increase in the speed of fast food through the pre-cooking and pre-assembly of hamburgers and related

foods, in state-of-the-art semi-automated hamburger assembly plants in Latin America and the Indian Subcontinent, via
a fleet of what some wag called the *Burger Bombers* on the
financial pages until we put a stop to those articles. We have
set an industry record not likely to be challenged for the
speed with which we are able to convert equatorial grassland
on the site of former useless impenetrable jungle into beef
patties and into hamburgers, and the speed with which we
can wrap and box and pallet the finished hamburger. We now
supply nearly thirty-seven percent of the fast-food outlets in
the major metropolitan areas of the country with our burgers, which skid down the chutes quite as if they were cooked
in the virtual kitchens backstage, as it were, from which are
emitted digital sounds of frying and genetically engineered
cooking odors. The return flights of our fleet of—well, why
not?—Burger Bombers are filled with biodegradable waste
products from these same fast-food outlets which are specially treated in separate wings of our burger assembly
plants, producing a palatable and nutritious food supplement
for the next generation of free-range beef cattle and chickens and hogs and farmed fish. I can't begin to list the labor
and tax savings of these offshore operations, not to speak of
the relief from so-called environmental regulations, the sum
total of which have resulted in both plummeting prices and
soaring profits.

The Burger Bomber system was one of those little
unexpected gifts from my *General Theory of Mobility*, specifically from the proposition that posits that the more anything
and everything and everybody moves, the greater the profit

margin, against all reasonable expectations. Only a few years ago it was calculated that farm produce traveled a mere 1,500 miles from field or orchard to table. Today the average hamburger flies nearly 7,000 miles from factory to little plastic table.

Now that, my little ones, is progress with a capital P.

23. 1:18 SCALE 1991 FERRARI 400L TURBO

I HAD NO SOONER FINISHED CHATTING WITH YOUR mother Deedums on the phone about your grandmother's recent bizarre behavior and was settling into my bed when the captain informed me that he's going to have to make an unscheduled landing in Honolulu owing to some pressure irregularities in the hydraulic system. He's already lined up, good man, either a Learjet or a 767 to get me to Chicago in time for an important evening meeting. The 767 is rather badly appointed, he said, but it would get me there quicker.

On the occasion of Groundhog Day, I have somewhat reluctantly offered you, Fabian and Rowena, an Italian custom-made model of my red 1991 Ferrari 400L Turbo, whose V-12 locked up on me on the Ohio Turnpike at 110 miles per hour and then disintegrated, throwing the car into a spin which eventually stabilized into a backward slide that subsequently gutted the eight-speed transmission and caused the car to pile backward into a bridge abutment, fortunately padded with huge yellow drums of sand. I walked away unscathed, but the westbound lanes of the turnpike were closed for three hours to remove other cars disabled by the Ferrari's disintegrating engine, transmission, and running gear parts. Needless to say I was enraged at the cost of replacing the entire engine and drive-train—which had to be custom-fabricated from scratch and was not covered by insurance—which came to just under $400,000. I sold the car like a hot potato. And have attempted to obliterate all traces of it from my memory, but unsuccessfully, as you can see. So let it serve as a warning.

You should probably pretend that there's nothing unusual about your grandmother's new so-called living arrangements, although it might be useful for you to suggest—*from the mouths of babes*, though you are both putting on height—that living in a tent down in the pasture is probably against the zoning laws of Fairlawn-Fairview Lake Village—even though we are technically not within the village boundaries. Technically it is the other way around as several obscure covenants make clear: Fairlawn-Fairview Lake Village and Fairlawn-Fairview Lake Village Estates, plus Langston Farm and Turf Estates, are all part of Fairview-Fairlawn Lake Manor, and any and all improvements are subject to the approval of the owner of the Manor, namely me, though I have never personally vetoed any such improvements—only my lawyers have. At any rate, you will probably not understand, fortunately, her prattle about *living lightly on the land* and refusing to ever again drive a car. She will soon enough discover what going shopping on foot to Fairlawn-Fairview Lake Village will involve, if she takes a direct route, cutting through heavy-duty field fencing with bolt cutters a mile down the pasture and then scaling a brick wall topped in razor-wire (made by a branch of her own family, coincidentally) and then wandering around the curving streets for at least a mile to Pâté & Pâté in the Village where she will have a world-class choice of pâtés, plus one local and two national newspapers.

I suppose this has been a long time coming, and I suppose I have chosen to ignore the signs or have simply not seen them because I have been away so much on business travel and so single-minded at building the family fortune into an impregnable fortress, and because of this I have tended to believe that her pining for *the simple life* was one of those themes she chooses to bring up whenever she feels the need to aggravate me, usually just after I get back from somewhere like Bombay, Jakarta, or Cape Town. She did not react well over dinner last week when I said, *If you want to live lightly on the land we can hire a hot-air balloon*, which amused you a little too much, Fabian, to the point that we had to excuse you from the table, suggesting that you take your giggling and hiccups elsewhere.

I have ordered a tent, she said.

A tent? Whatever for?

I'm moving into a tent down in the field, she said, looking down at her plate.

A tent? A tent? What will the neighbors say? A foolish question: we have no neighbors within two miles.

I want to live simply, she said. *On a little air mattress, in a little sleeping bag, with a little stove to heat tea on.*

Where did you ever get such insane ideas? Another foolish

question. Obviously she was hankering for a return to our old newlywed camping days of long ago, having mentally airbrushed away the bugs and mud that had once put a damper on her notions of the *simple life*.

From this little catalogue I've ordered it all from.

A thought flashed through my brain. I could call my friend who runs the FBI and see if they couldn't seize the shipment. Impound the UPS truck as evidence of a plot. Filled with camping gear and possibly even explosives. Very suspicious, I could hint.

She went on with a wave of the hand around our dining room. *I'm so tired of all this.*

What? Tired of the one-ton chandelier, assembled out of 4,424 separate crystals, which took seven weeks to correct a westward list and hang properly? Tired of the oriental rugs rolled and dragged and no doubt probably stolen along the way from the far corners of the Orient? Tired of the inlaid *Troisième Empire* dining table that when fully extended can seat thirty-six? Tired of the Barbed Wire Robber Baron's silver service made from an especially pure vein of Bolivian silver? How could she be tired of the very things that exhilarate me through their heft, their weight, their bulk, their polish, their woof and warp, their fine details, their wonderful complexity, their rarity, and their preciousness? How could she be tired, except perhaps physically, or strolling through or hiking up and down the hallways, upstairs and downstairs, and in and out of 120 perfectly furnished rooms and the seventeen galleries housing all my collections?

And this little plastic solar-heated shower thing you hang from a tree. And a cute little portable potty thing. She was becoming dangerously radiant, lifting her eyes and sweeping the table defiantly. Rowena, you were far too rapt.

I see, I said. *So when is all this happening?*

Tonight. I'm moving there tonight. And with a slow dramatic gesture she swiveled around in her chair and pointed to the French windows. Indeed, there it was, a corner of the green tent peeking out from behind a chestnut tree, a hundred yards down the field beyond the lawn.

At this point your mother Deedums finally spoke up. *But Mother you can't be serious. Rain, snow, ice. It's been a lovely February but—*

There are things for that in the catalogue.

Your father, fortunately, was silent as a stone. Had he said a single word, even *Pass the butter, please*, I would have removed the Barbed Wire Robber Baron's Colt .45 from the gun case in the hall and shot him dead. And then calmly carved a fourth notch in the wooden butt with a steak knife. The three others were business rivals, according to the Delahunt family lore that comes out after a few bourbons.

I completed our Sunday dinner without further comment as I was deep in mental calculations about where to set up various telescopes and infrared spotting scopes from either the upstairs bedroom window or my study windows next door and wondering how and when exactly I should or should not ask your grandmother whether her new *simple life* would permit the laying down of a phone line to her tent or whether she would take her cell phone with her—or whether I should simply let her solve these problems as they came to her.

I offered brandy with coffee but there were no takers except me. Nonetheless I raised my hand and offered a guileless smile along with a toast:

Happy Groundhog Day!

24. 1:24 SCALE 1992 LINCOLN TOWN CAR STRETCH LIMOUSINE

ANOTHER ONE I HAVE DEBATED NOT INCLUDING BUT have included owing to its worth as an example of the folly of social pressure. Are you surprised, my little ones, that someone who has reached such a pinnacle of success is subject to *what other people think*? What you will not realize for some years is that *prominence* is largely a matter of managing what other people think. I refuse to calculate the hours I waste each week posing for photographs. For someone of my stature, this is the work of a staff of twenty, who in this particular situation issued a strong recommendation, virtually an order, that I purchase the longest Lincoln Town Car Stretch Limousine ever to be made, by three inches, because they believed that my official car, the 1980 Ford Fairmont Station Wagon, even if armored and provided with a supercharged V-8 engine, was beginning to be spun in odd and unpredictable ways by political cartoonists. And Howie, my driver of three years, was also reporting too many unsavory exchanges with other drivers while waiting for me outside restaurants and hotels, particularly on Manhattan's Upper East Side.

This was nothing compared to the public relations nightmare occasioned by Dierdre's tent and her so called seclusion in the pasture known as Martha Washington's Nap, where her friends began flocking to her in droves and even camping out at night with her. Martha Washington reputedly paused there for an afternoon nap in 1793 under the now-vanished elms. Something about the main route being flooded and the party having to seek higher ground. The Fairlawn-Fairview Lake Village Council was unfortunately unwilling to ban low-level helicopter flights—too many CEOs fly to work from their back yards—despite my sizeable contribution for a new clubhouse swimming pool. In desperation I had to call an old friend at the CIA and have him extend a no-fly corridor out from the nearby air base, which the agency runs under some fictitious name. But by then the damage was done and her little tent city and the golf carts that she used for ferrying her friends from the parking area in front of the Manor down across the grass had become the subject of photos spread out all over checkout stands throughout the nation, I have been told, and indeed the world—except in Pâté & Pâté in Fairlawn-Fairview Lake Village. Including scurrilous doctored photographs showing older women with obviously too young bodies allegedly dancing on the grass. I do not consider these photos suitable for your young eyes but have saved them in the archives for the very distant future when we can all have a hearty laugh about the days of Deirdre's Folly.

Which, alas, shows no sign of abating. My security people have checked out the license numbers of all those who have visited her, old family friends I am surprised have chosen to be so disloyal to me and have not even asked my permission to tramp, or roll, across the grass. I have been rendered singularly helpless here by the fact that the property is half in Deirdre's name. Anyway, I have sent my lawyers out to hunt down and punish the inventors of the utterly false headline, BILLIONAIRE LEON TUGGS SENDS WIFE OF FORTY YEARS OUT TO PASTURE, and another one, just for good measure, THINGIE SPOUSE SEEKS HOME ON THE RANGE. I have also sent my investigators to try to infiltrate the organization which seems to have sprung up out of Deirdre's ill-considered gesture, all on its own, and which has already set up offices in New York and Washington, offensively and possibly illegally appropriating our pasture's name, *Martha Washington's Nap*. It seems to be promoting the insidious idea that if women would scrutinize their investments they could change the world "for the better." But of course any fool knows that if, in a moment of misguided equal-opportunism, our engineering and industrial establishment were turned over to women to manage and operate for a just day or a week, not to speak of a whole year, the entire world would come to an instant halt.

I appreciate, Rowena, your fey little reports on what's going on down at the *tents*—seven at last count—and how it is so much more fun sleeping on the freezing ground in sleeping bags and hearing the pitter-patter of rain at night on the tent canvas. I have suppressed my expressions of outrage that your mother has allowed you to spend whole nights down there with your grandmother, endangering your health, I am sure, probably because your *liberal democrat* father has somehow twisted her arm. You tell me that the most recent tent is called a *yurt* and that it has become a combination bath house and kitchen, and that it's so warm and steamy that the women don't usually wear any clothes at all. Charming observation, little Rowena. I am surprised that you have not yet reached the age to be shocked.

In my recent night visit in a Hummer specially purchased for the occasion (it will be added to your collection in the appropriate sequence) I was shamefully rebuffed by several women who, had they been dressed properly instead of being bundled up in thick down jackets, I would have probably recognized, even in the rain.

I'm here to see my wife, I bellowed out the open window of the powerful rumbling machine. *Please tell her I am here.* I could not be sure, but one of them could have been your former third-grade teacher, Ms. Plummets.

She has asked not to be disturbed. She's meditating.

Meditating? I believe it's possible to stop meditating at any time. I believe I have even seen her do it, stopping meditating. Repeatedly I have seen her stop meditating. Please tell her I must see her.

No.

Whoever you are, I said, *I do not take* no *for an answer, particularly in matters regarding my own wife.* Whereupon they gave me what must be called funny looks and disappeared into the darkness, leaving me no choice but to lean on the horn between bouts of calling your grandmother's name out the window, in answer to which there was not her familiar voice but a rising crescendo of hostile drumming. By then it was raining so hard

I couldn't tell whether the Hummer was being pelted with clods of mud and turf—which I suspected. But enough, I said to myself, throwing the vehicle in reverse to back up the grassy slope. Progress was slippery but secure in the dark. This is a vehicle the United States Army has certified as being unstuck-able. Until a certain point where, on not particularly steep ground, it lost all traction and I could hear the tires singing as they spun on the wet and muddy grass. I switched on all exterior floodlights—which I should have done much earlier—to illuminate an area 360 degrees around the vehicle and was puzzled to see rising around me a white bubbly substance like a kind of inflating pillow. Too late did I realize it was laundry detergent, or rather the suds created by perhaps several boxes or buckets of laundry detergent spread out on the wet grass and in the grooves of my previous tracks, whipped to a rising foam by my deeply cleated but totally useless all-terrain Conquista-Terravanquish-Trak tires, which, at $700 a pop, are guaranteed stuck-proof at depths up to two feet. By the time I became fully aware of my plight, the Hummer was completely enveloped in suds. I feared suffocation. I opened the door and jumped, rather fell, into the now muddy suds. I will spare you the pain of describing the state of your grandfather just after midnight as he staggered inside through a side door of the Manor.

Happily I later obtained a full refund for the Conquista-Terravanquish-Trak tires when the vehicle was finally air-lifted out of the pasture. The event also inspired top-level inquests at Conquista-Terravanquish-Trak and at the Pentagon, resulting in the early retirement of three generals.

* * *

My dearest Rowena, I believe you are old enough to know the meaning of the term *practical joke* (an oxymoron if ever there was one) but I will nonetheless assume that you were serving as mere putty in the hands of others with their clearly malign intentions. As far as I can make out the path that led to a certain inflammatory pamphlet being placed on my dinner plate (I had just returned from yet another tiring trip to Tokyo and am back in the air heading yet one more time for Tokyo) by your maybe innocent hands probably began with one of the amazons at Camp Martha Washington's Nap—as the national press will now have it—and then led to your fourth grade class, or more exactly into the hands of your former instructor or minder or whatever, Ms. Plummets, who then—most likely—pressed into your sweaty little palms and those of all your playmates, male and female alike, packets of the pamphlets bound together with rubber bands, and instructions whispered into your innocent ears to the effect of *Go forth and ruin the world*. Well it certainly ruined my dinner. Some of that superb Japanese tuna I have helicoptered to the back door. What a waste. I can readily imagine your father egging you on. *Psst! Right there. On Grandpa's plate. Right in the middle. Hurry up, he's coming.* Although you now read quite well, happily most of this propaganda is over your head.

Of course I sat down and whipped out my napkin as if

there was nothing unusual at finding a rabble-rousing arch-feminist pamphlet on my dinner plate—or to be exact, on one of the Barbed Wire Robber Baron's dinner plates, Spode, I believe. I carefully unfolded my reading glasses. While seeming to read it carefully—I had no need to read it beyond the first line, WOMEN OF THE WORLD AWAKE—THE LONG NAP IS OVER—I amused myself by tabulating its grammatical and spelling errors, seventeen in number, which gave the impression of a slow and methodical perusal to your father and mother, who were watching me out of the corners of their eyes as they picked away at their salads. Identical pamphlets sat at various angles beside their plates. Your mother's appeared to have been folded and rumpled and then smoothed out again. To your credit, Fabian, you had turned yours into a paper glider, or into an attempt at one.

I seized upon the moment and pulled my chair up to yours. *What you need is more wing, Fabian, more wing surface. More surface equals more lift. It will also improve the balance so it doesn't nose dive quite so often. Just to be sure, you can add tiny ailerons to give it just the right additional amount of lift. Lift, Fabian, think lift. Lift, think lift even before you begin to fold the paper. Lift, Fabian, lift.*

With the remote, I ignited the fireplace log. The screen, as yet unmotorized, was still in place, however. I swept around the table and pulled it aside and then returned to my place and with a single swoop launched the paper glider across the Persian carpet and directly into the flames. With a little *poof* it was gone.

That was an excellent demonstration of the principle of lift, if I may say so myself, Fabian. To your credit, Fabian, you were appropriately entranced. I fixed my gaze upon your father. *Chippo, pass me over yours. I want to make sure that it wasn't just a fluke, that we have real lift here.*

Yes sir, he said with a grimace, handing it to you, Fabian, who passed it on to me. I never should have mocked his preference for calling me *sir,* which I now found music to my ears, particularly in the absence of other editorial comment. In a blink I folded the pamphlet into a slightly different configuration, tested the balance, tweaked the wings, and launched it toward the fireplace. It fell short on the brickwork in front but skidded under the gas log where it slowly turned brown before igniting.

Let's see if we can do better than that. Deedums? Without looking at me, Deedums handed over her pamphlet. Her swollen red eyes indicated she had been crying. Her mother's behavior was having the unfortunate effect of shaking her convictions about how the world was arranged, which were passable versions of my own convictions, that *men* make the world of things in order for it to be a workable place for *women,* who should busy themselves with *peopling* the world of men's *things.* She knew perfectly well that the Martha Washington's Nap movement sought to cut the world in half and throw the half it didn't like—*men and their things*—into the sea. With her pamphlet, I created yet a third design, which evoked a supersonic fighter plane with little bends at its wing tips. I sailed it straight into the flames. *Poof!*

And Rowena? Come on, now. But you, little Rowena, or rather not-so-little-anymore Rowena, your cupid lips having—when did this happen?—evolved into a swollen pout and your round saucer blue eyes having acquired a squinting edginess, you slowly pulled the pamphlet off the table and turned and gave your mother the coldest look I have ever seen come out of you.

Which of course I ignored. *Oh,* I said, *I forgot my own.* Which I quickly folded up into a complicated four-wing model, launching it vigorously into the fireplace in a down-swooping to up-swinging arc. It disappeared briefly up the chimney before falling back down into the gas logs and bursting into flames. *Poof!* Not for nothing was I given a prize at the end of my senior year in engineering school for having successfully launched more paper gliders in Riles Lecture Hall—traditional signal to lecturers that they were becoming boring and repetitious—than any other student. The Cement Glider (Class of '58) has been my prized paper-weight ever since. Which is why it occupies the position of honor in the gallery devoted to displaying my world-class collection of paper gliders signed by famous personages.

But the vigor of my swing, or the twisting movement of my torso, sent my left elbow into the stemmed crystal water glass, which fell over with a thump, and we all watched silently as the water fanned out under the lace table cloth.

After that, it was a quiet dinner at least. Probably for the best. As I chewed, I tried not to keep time with the sound of drums echoing up from Camp Martha Washington's Nap.

*   *   *

I suppose I should be proud in a way that you mastered the security code to my upstairs studio door, Fabian—your cousin Barton Delahunt is far too doltish for that—though I must express my censure in no uncertain terms for you having chosen to become peeping Toms by means of my binoculars and telescopes set up on tripods. Your flushed faces and giggles as you were bending over to look through the lenses while trying to keep your balance on the footstools you had dragged over to the bay window to get a better view over the treetops, before you noticed my unexpected presence, occasioned by an early return from Moscow—your smirks gave the lie to your too glib excuses—*We just wanted to see Grandma* —as I chased you two out of my study. And see much more, I am sure. A quick glimpse through the glasses confirmed my suspicions. There was quite a bit of shameless nude sunbathing down there on this unseasonably warm early spring afternoon. Had I been able to instruct you on the intricacies of Industrial Sex, you could have dismissed this mass display of pussies and breasts—I could swear they were all pointed deliberately in the direction of the Manor—as scarcely titillating at all and would have used the binoculars and telescopes as I do, to seek for developments of a strictly political nature. After a careful scanning of the scene, I found none. Being a weekday, the gathering had dwindled to its hardcore group of a hundred or so.

But finally—and reluctantly—I resolved to call the county health department in person, claiming to be a simple landowner. I rarely do anything in person except drive, fly, or boat. But this time I decided to make an exception. I called and introduced myself and complained about the unauthorized encampment in my lower field going under the name of Camp Martha Washington's Nap.

Well, Mr. Tuggs, we've been treating it as a private reception, said the earnest voice of a young *liberal democrat* civil servant, so called.

A private reception that goes on for thirty-seven days? A private reception that goes on for thirty-seven days and nights? A reception that swells to nearly a thousand over weekends? Features nude sunbathing by day and drum beating and bonfires by night? A private reception, you say? I would like you to explain in detail your definition of a "private reception."

Well I believe, Mr. Tuggs, we have all the requisite permits for whatever goes on there, obtained by—*one moment please.* There were some rumbling noises and he then came back on the phone and tentatively read out my Deirdre's name. I could have guessed this in advance. *This is your wife, am I correct, Mr. Tuggs?*

Who else do you think she is?

No one, Mr. Tuggs. But as co-owner of record of Fairlawn-Fairview Lake Manor she has taken out the requisite permits for what she describes on the form as a permanent private reception.

And you accepted that?

No Mr. Tuggs, I did not. The approval was signed by Thea

Westheim, the county health director, who I believe is at the reception *as we speak. We haven't seen her in the office for days.*

I slammed down the phone and reminded myself never to do anything in person ever again. The terrible thought occurred to me that I might be losing my touch. I went back to the telescope, hoping to find a clue how to end this backyard insurrection. National Guard? Pinkertons? A good blizzard would do it in a flash, of course.

Damned global warming.

25. 1:8 SCALE 1953 INDIAN BLACK HAWK CHIEF MOTORCYCLE WITH SIDECAR

ON THE OCCASION OF THE TENTH ANNIVERSARY OF Thingie® Corporation International's gross sales having attained $10,000,000,000, I am adding these 1:8 scale prairie-green 1953 Indian Black Hawk Chiefs to your collections—the original of which I purchased ten years ago, on the signal date in question, though I believe I have only ridden the bike on public holidays on three or four occasions, accompanied by two armed bodyguards on Harleys and a surgeon with expertise in emergency medicine on a Honda, and a mechanic expert in antique Indian motorcycles on his Suzuki, followed by my caterer in a stretch GMC Suburban owned by the company—all at the insistence of your grandmother Deirdre, who fainted when I took her out onto the front verandah for her first look and gestured toward the magnificent machine parked in the shade of the circular front drive. Often we were honored by an ad-hoc police escort. Behind my dark goggles and under my safety helmet, I was no doubt mistaken for the President, or a former President, and I waved accordingly.

The ten-billion-dollar mark, which corresponded

coincidentally with the harvesting of our first million acres of timber, was the first credible index—to the skeptics—that Thingie® Corporation International actually had some hope of conquering the market. This finally put to an end what one might call the "paper tiger" phase in which critics had been dismissing the Thingie® as a flash in the pan, the Hula Hoop of home and office products, here today and gone tomorrow. I could go on and on, listing all the words and phrases and sound bites that critics of the Thingie® have since had to sit down and eat plain and raw, even as they try to distract themselves by re-arranging all the Thingies® and Thingamabobs® on their desks.

These same critics have of course seized upon Camp Martha Washington's Nap with all the fury of sharks held too long on vegetarian diets and are now indulging in orgies of speculation, particularly about the state of my soul in this time of crisis. *What must it feel like*—their favorite phrase—to be the third richest man in the universe and have your wife of forty years plotting revolution in your lower field with a bunch of half-naked (actually fully unclothed, weather permitting) *amazons*? Happily they don't know old Deirdre. They don't know that she's probably more like the queen bee, just sitting there and enjoying all the fawning and atten-tion, now and then shifting a thigh in order to lay an egg. Do I miss her? Damned right I do. Who wouldn't miss a woman who every single morning of our married life—she does this on the phone when I'm traveling on business—checked that all my shirt and suit buttons were properly buttoned and made sure the zipper on my fly was up and the belt through all the loops and my tie properly cinched up, and who said goodbye every morning with a little chant, *Spectacles, testicles, wallet, watch—everything on board?* I am not good at either dressing or eating, always a sign of brilliance.

It was therefore with the greatest of reluctance that I rummaged through Deirdre's motorized walk-in closets and, almost averting my eyes, chose a flowing green full-length coat and a large green hat with a veil, which at least would go well with the prairie green paint job of the Indian. By wrapping the coat around my pinstripe suit I intended to create an impression from a distance, not close up, in order to gain entrance into the inner sanctum of Camp Martha Washington's Nap and have a little chat with my wife at last. The hat was certainly a finishing touch. I strode downstairs and out into the garage, recently expanded from seven to eighteen stalls, at the far end of which was parked the somewhat neglected Indian. But tires were firm, there was a full tank of gas and no oil drips on the floor, so I opened the fuel shut-off and set the choke and gave the machine a few priming kicks—and amazingly it fired up, with a cloud of blue smoke. I back-walked it out of the garage and then headed down the drive, veil lowered over my face. I was vaguely under the impression that shouts of *Hey, you* were coming from behind, but a running figure in the rear-view mirror was a vibrating blur. Probably one of my mechanics.

It is at times like this I quite forget who I am, which is fine, and others do too, which is not. Having neglected to repeat Deirdre's morning litany, I had left behind my wallet and a remote signaler for the gate house, and so I was flagged to a halt by the security guard, where my getup caused dozens of journalists and cameramen to look up from their morning coffee. As I lifted my veil and shouted through clenched teeth, *It's me, idiot,* I could hear car and van doors slamming and the slap of shoes hitting the asphalt. The guard, a new one, froze in utter panic, forcing me to skid to a halt just in front of the still-closed gate and to back-walk the machine a few paces, whereupon I dropped it into low and gunned it through a privet hedge to the right. My personal motorcycle restorer will not like this, I thought, as I heard the branches scratch past, just before everything went blank.

The rest, like billions of others, I was able to watch from the comfort of my hospital bed. Broken collarbone, cracked ribs, sprained ankle. As, plunging through the hedge, Deirdre's green coat became entangled in the chain and was ripped from my back, causing me to lose my balance and come down with a thud on my left side while the machine proceeded on without me for some distance until it crashed into the NBC van. The doctor said that Deirdre's hat saved me from concussion or worse.

Headlines, headlines. They are tediously familiar by now, from the cruel TUGGS: DRAG QUEEN OF HIGH FINANCE to the more compassionate BEREFT TUGGS DOFFS DISGUISE TO ABDUCT SPOUSE, FOUNDER OF RADICAL FEMINIST MOVEMENT.

Of course they could have put a HEROIC in there somewhere.

26. 1:100 SCALE 1993 BOEING 737

THESE ARE ACTUALLY THE SECOND 1:100 SCALE MODELS of the first personal Boeing 737 I purchased. I sent back the first set when I discovered the manufacturer was employing *union labor* in some of its operations, the point of which will become evident shortly, my dear little ones. When you pull the tail in a backward direction, the roof of the plane pops open and reveals from aft to fore the galley, the dining area, living room, the bath, and my sleeping quarters, with a tiny model of me sitting at the dining room table with a phone to my ear. I know you enjoy visiting me in the hospital but I frankly did not find the experience profitable—of being in the hospital. I particularly missed my habitual hours in the air. Other than your two visits, which allowed me to appreciate how you have both become all elbows and knees and arms and legs of startlingly smooth skin and with your mother's large even white teeth, having been, both of you, spared your father's moray-eel-like mouth and small teeth.

These latest additions to your collections are to celebrate my release from medical confinement and my return to Fairlawn-Fairview Lake Manor, where, from my second floor study, I will resume direction of Thingie® Corporation International and its multitude of subsidiaries until I am able to more easily return to my weekly commute to our Chicago headquarters and less regular but frequent visits to our twenty-eight regional and nineteen global nodes. My mission on my 1953 Indian to rescue your grandmother and to disband the illegal gathering having failed, I am once again presented with the mournful spectacle of the encampment several hundred yards down the south field out the bay windows of my study. You are probably dying of curiosity—or will at the appropriate age—to know the nature of the conversation between your mother and me in my hospital suite, during those few moments we sent you off to be taken care of by my bodyguards; so for the sake of posterity, more of which below, I have recorded the gist of our remarks.

I finally saw her, Deedums said softly, settling herself in a chair beside my bed, after having nudged closed the door. There have already been three attempts to penetrate hospital security by media.

What does she want?

She wouldn't say. She just referred me to her "spokeswomen."

She's being held captive against her will, I'm certain of it. The long and the short of it is that they've kidnapped her and are holding her captive against her will. She's a hostage, in short.

Yes, Father. Deedums was silent for a moment. Then she looked up. *But you have to remember that Mother also used those words with a little laugh and a shrug when——well, when I was lit-tle. All the time.*

So what? I shot back. *She could come and go whenever she liked. I regularly said to her, go shop in New York, London, Paris, Milan. Did she ever go? No, of course not. And why? Because she was pathologically addicted to thrift stores, which was fine during the early days of all that litigation, but later——I never knew why she kept going to them. What did her so-called spokeswomen have to say for themselves?*

She ignored my question. *Mother once told me that was the only way she could know how ordinary people lived. She could touch their lives in the racks of old clothes and all those shelves of old crockery and kitchen appliances and——*

I interrupted: *I wouldn't know about any of that. And it's all nonsense anyway. All she had to do was open the phone book and pick a name at random and call them and say, "Hello, I'm calling to talk to an ordinary person to see how you live." Simple. We've had this conversation a dozen times before, down to the very word. What does she want? What besides old clothes and old pots and pans? She must want something. What is it? They should ban thrift stores for undercutting the real economy. I'll buy her as many thrift stores as she wants. I'll put a thrift store at the end of the drive, if that's what she wants.*

Father. . . . There was something different about your mother, something about the eyes and mouth, a sort of slackening from the fixed and focused and cool calculating courtroom look of a successful attorney in charge of corporate litigation against disgruntled consumers, a new resemblance to your grandmother, very slight, almost imperceptible, a sort of softening. An awful thought darted through my brain. Had your father finally infected her with the *liberal democrat* virus? Would she too soon turn against me? Or rather, I tried to reassure myself, was she allowing a measure of compassion to surface at the sight of me her father in lower leg cast and chest and head bandages and the thought of her mother being held hostage by radical feminist amazons at Camp Martha Washington's Nap?

My little Deedums, these are trying times, I ventured, hoping to turn the conversation to a more promising direction. *Murphy's Law has come home to roost. I have been reviled in the national press. Only this morning I was forced to read a review of a book in the* Times *called* Thingie® Unbound, *or some such.* In it my old college roommate Ralphie Fitch purports to know the whole truth about my undergraduate days and the founding of Thingie® Corporation International. He alleges all kinds of predatory business practices which rocketed it to the position of being the third largest corporation in the world in only thirteen years, with gross sales larger than the economy of all of Austria, or is it Australia? I could have gone on and on but didn't. The bandages were beginning to chafe.

Deedums looked down and opened her purse and pulled out a piece of paper and unfolded it. *These are their demands.*

Your mother's?

No. Theirs. The organization's. I doubt she knows or even cares. I understand she's said something like, Take my name and use it however you like.

She looked down at the paper for a long moment and then slowly passed it over to me. My eyes stayed perfectly in focus as they bounced down the list, one item at a time. *Uniform international minimum wage. Free global movement of labor. Uniform international environmental standards. Uniform international health care, child care, senior care. International uniform reproductive*—and so on and so forth, ad infinitum, ad nauseam, crackpot ideas all, which would spell the end of capitalism as we know it, the end of the profit motive, and the end of wealth in the hands of the wealthy. And meaning for you, my little ones, the ripping away of a comfortable protected life and reducing you to the status of near penniless shoppers shuffling up and down the aisles of giant megamall thrift stores. Because that's all that would be left.

I can't begin to list the things that would be swept away in such a world. Your grandmother's *simple life* indeed, come home with a vengeance. My error here was that after the episode in the woods I don't know how many decades ago, perhaps we should have kept going *camping* more often when we were a still fit young couple and worked harder at surviving cold nights on the hard ground and perfecting the business of eating salads of grass and preparing grasshopper stir-fries.

Had I had two functional hands I would have folded the paper into a useful glider and shot it under the door and down the hallway.

Instead, I handed it back to Deedums and said, *Nowadays I believe they recycle this sort of thing.*

Our talk was interrupted—and in effect concluded—by a call from my scheduling secretary wanting to start penciling in appointments following my planned release from the hospital the next morning.

27. 1:12 SCALE 1994 CHEVROLET SUBURBAN ALL WHEEL DRIVE STRETCH

FORTUNATELY THE PRAYED-FOR BLIZZARD ARRIVED TWO weeks into spring, concluding with a wonderful ice storm, which sent the encampment slipping and sliding and eventually packing, leaving nine dumpsters and thirty-eight Port-a-Potties I feared I would be billed for. But the FBI has assured me that they would take care of everything through WASTE/AMERICA Inc., which I understand is operated by the Bureau in order to ferret out suspicious activity by means of a thorough inspection of the nation's trash. They were probably already inside the encampment before the end, in the guise of Bicuspid Caterers, who provisioned the renegades during their final three weeks, to judge from some hints dropped by the director during several of our phone chats. The Bureau has generously offered to returf the entire lower pasture in May.

What Camp Martha Washington's Nap failed to understand is that *things* and the comfort and convenience they thrust into everyday life will always carry over *ideas*. It is clear that the winner in history is *things*. Instead of trying to change the world, from now on the masses will be obsessed with cleaning out their closets, garages, attics, basements, and storage units. *Thing* management, *thing* inventories, *thing* lists, *thing* dreams. And in order to manage their *things* the world has turned to that incomparable tool, the Thingie®, in such numbers as to defy all predictions, sending torrent upon torrent of the 1/100ths of a cent into the family treasure house. Men rule the world because they love *things*, and enough women love or tolerate men who love *things* to perpetuate the race. So another failed movement has been chased from the field and now squats on the back steps of the houses of power, awaiting an occasional distribution of crumbs. End of lesson. Or so I thought.

You two of course witnessed your grandmother's return to the high-ceilinged halls of Fairlawn-Fairview Lake Manor just as I did, since we were all sitting around the dining room table waiting for Flora to serve when Deirdre breezed in from the kitchen and sat down at her place quite as if nothing unusual had happened these past two months. She began prattling brightly about the wonderful new thrift store and soup kitchen she had found down in Baltimore, where she had luncheoned with the homeless, no doubt on one of her hopeless-cause junkets.

I must take you all there some day, she said.

Of course you must, I replied, noting she had made no comment on my ankle and chest braces. Her face was quite wind-burned, as if she had just come in from a long day of sailing.

At this point or earlier, I would have expected you two, my little pets, to thrust your bony gawky necks forward in her direction and call out such things as *Grandma, Grandma, tell us about what it was really like inside Camp Martha Washington's Nap* but in the sullen silence of the dinner table I detected a whiff of conspiracy. It rapidly became clear that Deirdre had conferred with you all separately or together, probably in the days of her re-emergence, and that possibly protracted negotiations had been conducted while I was away on business. Even my son-in-law Chip, never one to ignore an opportunity, stared at a distant object somewhere on the far side of the living room, perhaps a flying saucer, with too rigid indifference.

Excellent split pea soup, she went on. *I had Flora make it from organically grown peas.*

I see, I said.

They live so simply, those people.

Of course they live simply, the homeless, I said, warming to one of my favorite topics. *They have no homes, they have no things to speak of. They have no homes to put their things in, such as they are. In its infinite wisdom, our society has given those who have no homes to put their things in—it has given them the condition of homelessness. What could be simpler?*

The farmers, I mean.

Oh them. I wouldn't know.

We could sell the horses, she said. I could tell that the next big thing was ballooning up over her horizons. Of course we could sell the horses. A snap of the fingers and they're sold. They're plastic, life-sized horses. The groundsmen move them around before dawn each day, turning them this way and that, moving them into shade, or into sun, depending on the weather forecast. They help keep neighborhood real estate prices up in Fairlawn-Fairview Lake Village Estates for a fraction of the cost of live horses.

We could turn all the pastures into organic farm land, she said, finally turning to me and looking into my eyes for the first time in two months. *Martha Washington's Nap could manage it all.*

The chorus that followed this remark confirmed my suspicious.

What a wonderful idea, Deirdre, Chip observed a little too quickly. *Right out your window, a living little farm. An idea whose time has come.*

Can we have chickens? You, Fabian, of all people. *I always wanted chickens.* And what is this *we*?

And of course we must have rabbits. You, Rowena, knew not what you said.

Not to be outdone, I pitched in. *And what about pythons, lions. Alligators. We'll need to keep these populations in check. Nature is red in tooth and claw for a very excellent reason.*

Your mother put down her fork and leveled her gaze at me. *Father, it's a condition.*

Of course I could see it coming. The problem with the principle, *We do not divorce in this family, never have, never will* lies in the conditions imposed at certain periods throughout a long and extended marriage. This was Condition Number Six, by my reckoning. Number One, something about no partisan political arguments at family dinners, which unfortunately deprived these occasions of the spice and the sauce that made me salivate in advance at the prospect of nailing old Chippo. Number Two, something to do with off-color jokes. Number Three, something to do with what your grandmother tastelessly referred to as "the bimbos," details of which are best left unrecorded. Number Four required me to seek medical treatment for gas, so far unsuccessful. Number Five had to do with the establishment of separate bedrooms in the separate wings of the Manor and the protocols by which I was occasionally allowed to approach and enter hers, modeled, I suspect, on the Immigration and Naturalization Service regulations for undocumented workers attempting to enter the United States from Mexico. All this by way forewarning, young Fabian.

And just where is this play farm going to be, if I may ask? I demanded.

Deedums looked up and beckoned toward the high French doors. *The seventy-five acres between the house and the lake. Where the encampment was.*

Very well, I said, getting up from the table with a theatrical grimace. I turned and limped away. Then I turned and shouted back, *Call in the tractors,* before hobbling around the corner and up the stairs as slowly and as noisily as I could, huffing and puffing, instead of using the elevator.

As I say, young Fabian, be forewarned: no man ever expects his marriage to reach Condition Six. It happens even to the best of us—or for that matter especially to the best.

*   *   *

That was ten days ago. Happily I'm in the air again, comfortably curled up in my sofa at 30,000 feet, on the way to Taipei, trying to make up for lost time. That three weeks was the longest I've been uninterrupted on the ground in almost nine years, experience I hope to never have to repeat. Anything after two days, when I begin to itch to get back in the air, is almost unbearable hell.

This 1:12 scale model 1994 Chevrolet Suburban All Wheel Drive Stretch I presented to you both just before leaving was itself custom stretched the equivalent of the sixty-four inches the actual vehicle was extended. The occasion of the purchase of the actual vehicle, not the model, was the takeover of Gazillions Burgers by the Billions by Thingie® Corporation International and the creation of a new entity called Thingie®-Gazillions International. At no little cost, all this stretching, even the scale models. Though this was a personal car, I came to be known briefly as a stretch pioneer in the corporate world through commissioning other vehicles such as stretch crew-cab pickups, stretch Jeeps, stretch vans, and even stretch golf carts—to make it clear from a distance who was on the course. The 1994 Chevrolet Suburban All Wheel Drive Stretch was my preferred vehicle while visiting my collection of cattle ranches I had been quietly acquiring over the past several years in Wyoming, Montana, Idaho, and west Texas. Five virtually identical stretch Suburbans were commissioned for the ranches during 1994 and 1995. Because of the exorbitant cost of these custom-made scale models, Fabian and Rowena, I have only given you one each, not five, with me behind the wheel in a ten-gallon hat. At least they got the hat right.

Through accounting procedures I cannot possibly hope to explain, I am able to write off the operation of my five cattle ranches to Thingie®-Gazillion International in a most attractive way, to the benefit of your eventual portfolios, which will be nicely balanced with two and a half million acres of scenic real estate each upon my departure from the world. Your grandmother claims the only way she can tell one ranch from another is by the hardness or softness of the beds. Rather than try endlessly and pointlessly to explain the differences to her, I reluctantly adopted her naming system: The Low Hard Bed Ranch; the High Hard Bed Ranch, where you, Rowena fell off that horse; the Waterbed Ranch; the Sagging Soft Bed Ranch; and Rancho Insomnia—something about night owls and coyotes right under the window. And where you, Fabian, found a diamondback in your cabin under the bed. Not that Deirdre goes to any of them anymore.

But though I have moved up to be the second largest private landowner in the country, I still squirm at the thought of turning the lovely south-slope lawns and pastures of Fairlawn-Fairview Lake Manor into a manure-strewn *organic farm*. Indeed, I weep.

Take note of this, my little bunnies whom I used to

love to see in your fuzzy pajamas as you jumped up and down on the way upstairs to bed, on those rare evenings I was allowed into your parents' home, and before you got too adolescent shy to be seen in fuzzy pajamas.

Be that as it may, take note of this: your grandfather weeps. This is a historic event.

Once again, my little Fabian, or less little Fabian, because I see you have started to grow into your father's gangly hatchet-faced structure, though somewhat improved by a much better set of teeth, good Delahunt teeth—and thank god without his short little legs—once again we must have one of our little man-to-man talks about the relations between the sexes. By the way, I was able to catch the last few minutes of your soccer match, which I nearly missed owing to the usual delay trying to get out of Dallas-Fort Worth and by having to make a slight detour over the newly completed Thingie®-Gazillion Spire in the Loop, which my architect insisted I do during this first clear day since its completion. I was impressed by your running speed but a little disturbed at how you seem to avoid the action around the ball, failing utterly to make contact with it during my brief presence at the end. To her credit, your mother Deedums insisted you had actually kicked the ball twice and had, fortunately unseen by the umpire, kicked another player in the behind. And of course it was good to see you with blond hair all tousled and cheeks flaming red from the exertion.

Or imagined little talks because at your still tender age

you are only just becoming aware of the vast unknown territory that spreads out before you and which offers so many opportunities for confusion, ambush, embarrassment, disgrace, and fiasco. Even the very small handful of men who throughout history have attained the sort of pinnacle of success that I have—they have still been bedeviled by the question. Unless they have simply tried to ignore it, as I so often have. Yet sooner or later, at any age, at all ages, pressures build and build. A useful engineering analogy might be the teakettle whose stopper is completely sealed after it has been filled with water and placed on a burner, turned up high when young, low when old, or older. The water inside simmers away slowly and languidly, quite pleasantly at first, and then slower or faster becomes hot and begins to expand as it approaches boiling temperatures. Either way things eventually reach the bursting point.

As they did the other night between your grandmother and me. Well, I can't speak for her. *I* had reached the boiling point. Foot brace off, chest brace off, I was ready to go. Owing to my often all night telephone calls needed to keep in touch with Thingie®-Gazillion, our bedrooms, hers in the south wing, mine in the new north wing, are separated by a very long hallway. Having straightened things out nicely in Prague, emergency cell phone in my bathrobe pocket, I emerged at midnight from my bedroom and strode resolutely down the hall and turned the corner and marched the width of the second floor, and turned the corner and came to a halt before my wife's bedroom door.

Sex, I called out, *it's time for sex, my dear. Please open your* door, my dear, so that I may enter and we can have some sex. *Recreational sex? Athletic sex? Industrial sex? Wet sex? Dry sex? You name the sex, my dear, and we will have it—even all five if you wish.* I find it useful, which I offer as a tip, Fabian, to contemplate the inner workings of a 1937 Cadillac V-16 engine as its twin banks of pistons rise and fall in sequence, in the steel cylinder sleeves of its cast-iron block, while I am at work in these labors. But if you can't get off on that, think about how the oil pump works. *Come, come, my dear, let's not be shy or coy, it's time once again for sex, spelled S-E-X. Let's go for the S, let's go for the E, but let's especially go for the X. Yoohoo, sex time, Deirdre.*

After another ten minutes of my love calls—an approach favored by large mammals, science assures us—I am quite indefatigable at this hour—though I was once summarily thrown out of a hotel in Kuala Lumpur before I could explain that I had quite forgotten where I was, owing to time-zone-induced confusion—which held up their Thingie® licensing agreements for more than three years until I was finally issued an official apology—I heard the lock click and then, miracles of miracles, the door slowly swung open.

The point I'm trying to make for you, Fabian, is that if at first you don't succeed, just keep trying. Sooner or later they're bound to give in.

One more thing. When it rains it pours. I have just thrown down in disgust little Ralphie Fitch's second piece of trash, his unauthorized biography *Feet of Clay, Toes of Steel: How Thingie International Price-Fixed, Gouged, and Litigated Its Way to Global Dominance: Another American Success Story.* I ordered my chief steward to tear it into little bits and open a hatch and scatter it over the Atlantic. From the very first line, when he quotes some old wives' tale to the effect that behind every great fortune lies a great crime, to the very last line of the last footnote, it is all pure unmitigated garbage. Worse, the other night I could have sworn that your father Chip stuffed a copy behind his back while sitting in his fireside armchair just as I rounded the corner into your living room, which explains why for the first time in thirteen years he did not stand up with his usual distasteful grimace and limp *liberal democrat* handshake. He offered me two faux-deferential *sirs* instead. And eyes too wide, too bright.

And how are we this evening, sir? he chattered. *Collarbone still sending out those shooting pains? Finally bring the Chinese around, did you? Pleased with the market today, sir?*

Of course I'm pleased whenever the market adds two billion to my net worth. Who wouldn't be? *Very chatty you are tonight, Chip.*

Be that as it may—it's a free country and your father can read anything he wants, though it may cost him dearly in the end. I took umbrage in particular at chapter five about our undergraduate years and little Ralphie Fitch's tendentious version of the rivalry between the third-floor Wrist-Pin Society, of which I was a founding member, and the fourth-floor Crankshaft Group, to which he briefly belonged before being, please note, dishonorably expelled for his miserable and possibly failed performance. This was in the days before anyone had even thought up the idea of coeducational dormitories. As a result you had whole buildings filled with hot-blooded young engineers each with his teakettle about to explode.

Point of all this is that a true and unbiased account of these activities is a chapter in my privately printed *Manual of Industrial Sex*, all copies of which have been secured in the basement vault of the archives wing of the Manor. You will receive one for your eighteenth year, the right age for such useful information. Or perhaps less useful to you than it would have been to me at that age, at a time when coeducational dormitories became the rage—leading unfortunately to the demise of the Wrist-Pin Society and its many rivals. Little Ralphie Fitch casts his chapter as a breathless exposé of the real meaning behind my generous endowment of the Wrist-Pin Society Chair of Advanced Internal Combustion Design—when the mundane fact of the matter was there were considerable tax advantages for doing so at that particular time.

As for those other rumors, innuendoes, half-truths, distortions, lies, outright fabrications, and fantasies—I comfort myself with the vision of them reduced to confetti, tumbling in the slipstream behind my 737, on the night of the full moon as I flew back from Paris, and sinking through the air until they hit the water, floating briefly, before heading for the bottom of the Atlantic. A comforting vision marred only by the chief steward's words to the effect that there was no hatch he could safely open while travelling at 550 miles per hour.

Nonetheless I ordered him to tear the pages one at a time into tiny pieces. And where I could see him doing it.

28. 1:8 SCALE 1995 BENTLEY TURBO RL SALOON

I T IS UNDER VARIOUS CLOUDS THAT I STRUGGLE TO anticipate with my usual joy my next birthday, another big one, and so soon. You may think that a man who has everything might be losing his taste at my age for more. But in fact I don't have *everything*, which is probably impossible. If I had *everything* nobody else would own anything at all, and as desirable as that might seem, I fear it's impossible. But between what I own and what everyone else still owns, there remains a large—if narrowing—gap in which to flex my wants and desires. Of course I continue to do just that. So what, my little ones, do you think your grandfather wants for his next birthday? But lest you worry, I have instructed your mother in this demanding task, to assist you in selecting a really *big* present for me.

The 1:8 scale models of the 1995 Bentley Turbo R I'm adding to your collections along with full-length glass display cabinets to house them in—no occasion I can think of, just sheer grandfatherly generosity—represent the car I arranged for the corporation to buy for me for my last big one five years ago. When I had it flown to Montana to test the top speed on a reputedly straight country road, I was very disappointed that it failed to reach its advertised top speed of 137 MPH by 21 MPH. I complained vigorously to the company, which tried to weasel out of its claims by suggesting that the 7,000-foot altitude may have been a factor. I thought they drove these things up Everest to test them, but apparently not. And some company underling they flew over from Crewe, England, to inspect the wreck had the temerity to suggest that I was going too fast as it was, given the effects of an unposted dip through a drywash, from which the five-thousand-pound sedan and I and my two bodyguards emerged airborne at 116 MPH. We were never able to ascertain whether all four tires blew out in the wash or when we came back to earth. In any case it came down like a pancake and hit with a gush of fluids (oil, antifreeze, transmission fluid, mineral oil) and all eight airbags deployed when all four wheels literally came off as we plowed through the sage brush. The whole underbody of the car was distributed randomly over about an acre. The insurance company sold what was left for salvage with less than 200 miles on the odometer. Boys will be boys, as we used to say back in engineering school.

At any rate, in warm anticipation of my next big one I was able to tolerate your father Chip's annual report to the family on the state of his law firm—the one occasion on which I allowed him to rub my face in the environment, so to speak, and get away with it, more or less. So during his pale knock-off of my grander annual presentations, I tried to think of other things—it was a magnificent wreck, I must say, and the whole thing was captured from the air by CNN—while he prattled on about whales, polar bears, elephants, rhinos, house mice, and English sparrows, the dropping out of the sky of which is now apparently cause for big bucks litigation. So with a benign smile fixed on my face and ears quite firmly closed as I recalled the post-mortem helicopter survey of the scene of the wreck—black tire marks on the leading edge of the dip and then a hundred feet or more of nothing and then the wide black smears where the tires touched down and then a succession of dark stains where the fluids emptied out over the pavement and then the raw track out into the sagebrush, a tangle of barbed wire and fence posts in its wake and the wheelless black hulk gleaming in the bushes—I believe the paint was called "Mason's Triple Black"—a magnificently crafted automobile despite its unfounded claims—when something your father said brought my senses back to the present and I decided reluctantly to pay attention.

I am restrained, he was saying, *by family loyalty from litigating against any of your holdings, sir, but I would suggest that you listen to a little bird perched at your ear which might be trying to say that Thingie®-Gazillions might soon experience a unique challenge by a certain labor union.*

Thanks for the tip, Chip.

Not a tip. I believe it might already have been filed, sir.

Where?

Not at liberty, sir.

Of course he knows perfectly well that all I have to do is call my friend who runs the *Journal* and find out what's going on. In fact I probably already knew what was going on but they just hadn't got around to telling me yet. But your mother wisely announced that dinner was about to be served and would we please adjourn to the dinner table and defer all business talk to coffee and brandy, for the sake of our digestion. And for the sake of the children.

After the usual difficult long silence which I was about to break with some random reflections on the state of your parents' grounds—driveway trees needing to be trimmed, grass growing in a crack in the pavement about a quarter mile down your driveway, weather vane arrow frozen pointing north—your grandmother Deirdre decided to make an announcement.

I've made a discovery, she said brightly.

And what might that be? I inquired.

I've seen my first junkyard.

First? Junkyard? I ventured. *Please explain, my dear. I am preparing myself to be fascinated.*

This lovely homeless woman down at the shelter needed a car, you see, she began with a little flush and a fluttering of hands, sure signs that she was taking up the banner of yet another lost cause.

Yes, there is a crying need among the homeless for cars. But since the homeless are also by definition garageless, we might be creating yet more social problems by giving them cars. So many *liberal democrat* programs are like that.

Please go on, I prompted.

And she said she could get one very cheaply at this junkyard place. "Would you like to go there?" she asked. "Why yes," I said, "I've never been to one of those." Her boyfriend told her about it, you see.

Her homeless but not carless boyfriend?

I think she told me he had just had his stolen, which is why I gave her a ride.

Proceed, I suggested. Given the rapt expressions on all your faces, Deirdre could as well have just returned from the moon.

So we arrive at this place, called something like Manny's Motors, and he shows her this nice car—

Which you buy for her? I hinted.

I helped her buy it, yes. But anyway, while she was filling out some papers I stood up and looked out the extremely dirty window, and there spread out before me was this most amazing collection of cars, some of them upside down and others laying on their sides, but what looked to me like perfectly good solid nice cars. My first thought was that there's something wrong with this.

More exactly, I corrected, *something very wrong with each and every one of them. That's why they're there. There's something wrong with them. They don't run. They don't start. They don't stop. They don't back up.*

After a little flurry of objections and explanations from your mother and father attempting to explain to your grandmother what she had in fact actually seen, as opposed to what she thought she saw, I tapped my water glass with my knife. *You didn't buy the junkyard, did you, Deirdre?*

She ignored my question, an ominous sign.

And on the way home I began thinking about all those cars sitting out there in that place—well, it was worse. I began noticing junkyard after junkyard on the way back to the shelter. Thinking about how each one had probably once belonged to some happy young couple with a couple of children, just like you Rowena and you Fabian, sitting in the back seat, with their dog. And then all of a sudden something terrible happened. And there they are, in the homeless shelter. And their cars in the junkyard. And their dog probably languishing in the animal shelter.

I see, I said.

Then it's simple, she said. *You must absolutely call up your friends in Detroit or wherever it is and tell them to stop making new cars, that there are plenty of perfectly good old ones to fix up.*

Right on, Chip suggested.

But if there were dots here, they were not connecting. If we fix up old cars for the garageless (never mind the consequences for the moment) then there will be no need to close down Detroit. If we close down Detroit, on the other hand, the supply of old cars will vanish, leaving the garage-less/homeless carless, just like they are now, fortunately.

Just tell me this, Deirdre, I said instead of laying out the theory of the marketplace for perhaps the hundredth time. *Did you buy the junkyard?*

Not exactly, she said while glancing down at her nails.

"Not exactly" suggests a clever subterfuge, my dear. Come on, out with it.

The shelter bought the junkyard.

With of course her money, which is also my money. Though the money she has available for her lost causes is based on a complex formula calculated to maximize on our so-called unearned Thingie®-Gazillion income, combined with her share of the resurrected Delahunt fortune.

Grandma, can I go see the junkyard? came your excited cracking voice, Fabian, at my left elbow.

And yours from across the table, Rowena: *Can I come too?*

Well, said Deirdre, quite pleased by the reception of her ideas among the younger generation, *why don't we all drive down and have a look?*

No thanks, I said with a florid gesture that brought my wristwatch within focus beneath my nose, *I have a call scheduled with the Prime Minister of Japan, thank you.*

By the time I had finally turned in at 3:00 A.M. I was still trembling at how little of the mechanisms of industrial civilization Deirdre had understood, despite all I had tried to teach her during our many long decades of marriage.

Use it up. Throw it out. Buy another one. That's what makes the world go round. From which it follows that if you don't use it up, don't throw it out, and don't buy another one, the whole damned system will fall apart.

And then you, my little grandchildren, will be stripped of all your so-called unearned income and will be out in the cold in the dark, rubbing two sticks together.

29. 1:12 SCALE 1996 BENTLEY TURBO RL 4-DOOR SALOON

OVERCOMING THE SHABBY WAY I WAS TREATED BY THE manufacturer, I ordered a second Bentley Turbo with all the options (sunroof, rear picnic tables, deluxe veneer, leather headliner) but when they realized who they were selling the car to they delivered it along with a factory rep who had the gall to refuse to turn it over without a factory-installed speed governor set at 100 MPH max. Had I not been so taken by the deep metallic maroon, I would have refused delivery. As it was, the hulking beauty and exquisite finish of the car inspired me to enlarge the living room at Fairlawn-Fairview Lake Manor to nearly twice its original size and install a full-size automated garage door behind a seventeenth-century Japanese screen, enabling me to drive the Bentley inside and park it on a specially treated Persian carpet so that I could enjoy its presence during the long evening hours I occasionally spent at home—even sit in the comfortable back seat reading the paper. This was to be the first car to be so honored in the household. Eventually, as you know, the living room was expanded again to accommodate three others, of which more at the proper time.

Your grandmother Deirdre was at first uneasy, as she is at any change.

It makes me feel, she remarked after dinner one night, *as if I'm having tea in a parking garage. What's to prevent one of them from just starting up and coming after us?*

But the cars, softly glowing under the warm light of the living room, brought back sweet memories of my childhood days when I wandered the streets of the Indiana town I grew up in not far from South Bend, in the 1940s and early 1950s. On the way home from school I would stop and press my nose to the plate-glass windows of automobile showrooms to gaze on the sharklike forms within, their chrome and glass gleaming in the semi-darkness. There was the Oldsmobile-Buick dealer, with slanted plate-glass windows, slightly tinted. And two blocks down, the Studebaker showroom with its green bullet-nosed cars made in South Bend itself; and a block the other way, the corner showroom of the Hudson dealer and cars painted in dark metallic tones with deep, shadowy grills; and across the street, Fords chromed up and flashy after the war. These were my childhood shrines, the forbidden sanctuaries of my future life as an owner of many, many cars.

And the Bentley—not the maroon Turbo RL, but its more recent replacement—is where tomorrow I will reluctantly consent to let you, Fabian, sit behind the inlaid walnut steering wheel, on your twelfth birthday, in the living room, and instruct you on which buttons to push and how to move the gear shift lever and the accelerator and brake pedals, with some theoretical pointers on steering

and cornering. I know you think you already know how to
drive, having successfully piloted your friend Christopher's
three-wheeler off the end of the dock down at the lake and
into sixteen feet of water, but permit me to suggest that
that brief experience should not be allowed to count. We
may even turn on the exhaust fan set in the living room
floor and start the car up and drive it a few feet between
the sofa and the Steinway and then carefully back, particularly if your grandmother has decided to go up to bed. You
need not make motor noises, as this car does not make
motor noises. It is quite silent except for the whoosh of its
fans and the thrum of the exhaust when you let up on the
gas—but you have probably passed beyond the age of making motor noises anyway. I trust you will take this exercise
seriously and that it will enable you to finally understand
the gravity of your recent pranks involving your collection
of models, and that it will lead to the end of those childish
days of such things as making the power windows go up
and down in order to see if they will decapitate your sister's dolls. You have reached the age in life, Fabian, to begin
imagining ahead to the time in three or four years you will
actually begin to drive a car. Practice makes perfect, and
practice starts early—just as if you were learning the piano
or violin.

　　You will be practicing, of course, not in order to
become a mere driver of cars and other vehicles or a pilot of
planes or even a captain of powerboats, but for something far
more important. You will be practicing to become a man, a
special kind of man far superior to all those that have come

before, those throwers of spears and rocks, those wielders of clubs and swords and firearms, petty smashers and break-ers—more of which below, by the way—and uprooters, defacers, and demolitionists. No, none of these will you become. They may be passing phases, of course, on the path to that far greater role of a fully-realized contemporary of the world, in its present magnificent configuration. You will become a *Petroleum Man*, and this is what you must now begin practicing for.

Although the concept of a *Petroleum Man* may at first seem frightening in terms of the awesome responsibilities implied in such a title, all you have to do is look up around you and you will see countless examples of exceedingly successful *Petroleum People,* namely myself and your grand-mother (though she doesn't know it) and your own moth-er and father (although he denies he is such a thing). What we *Petroleum People* are good at doing is arranging our lives and the lives of others so as to use as much petroleum and derivative products and related natural resources as is humanly possible, in order to create and use up more and more *things* of ever increasing complexity, and in order to replace the now clearly obsolete natural world with a model of vastly improved design—that is, a world faster, more convenient, more comfortable, and far more enter-taining than the rather shoddy model clapped together in six days. Petroleum was hidden away in the bowels of the earth so that when humanity reached that degree of evolu-tion where we finally deserved to use it, it would be there. Evolution being, please note, nothing more than nature's far too sluggish version of planned obsolescence.

Now about the incident last week, which I cannot pretend to ignore or condone. I am only hoping that putting you behind the wheel of the Bentley will wake you up to magnitude of your deed. I had thought that you had reached the age at which, in preparation for your initiation, I could allow you to handle as frequently as you wanted the nearly thirty items of your collection. As a result, over your father's irrational objections, I had installed in your room a custom-made cherry wood case with glass doors. No doubt I did not sufficiently anticipate the malign influence of your new best friend, Christopher Something. Burr, I believe. No one bothered to tell me about the bee-bee-shot hole in the plate glass window of my upstairs studio until too late. His family is high-rise construction money, never to be trusted.

From what I have pieced together of the events surrounding the near destruction of your collection down at the tennis courts, you and your little friend Christopher boxed up some twenty items in your collection and carried them down to the tennis courts one afternoon last week after school, before your parents had come home and while the servants were napping, shall we say, in the furnace room, where the heat had forced them to remove most of their clothing. There, on the clay of the court, you laid the precious car and truck and airplane models of your collection in what you called, whimpering, *a Desert Storm Enemy Convoy* and proceeded to fire on them with Christopher's beebee gun and an amazingly large cache of illegal firecrackers, rockets, cherry bombs, and at such close range that your wise-ass little friend had to have a chip of plastic extracted from his eye, though his sight was spared, for better or worse. In the rush to the hospital, clothing hastily restored to the servants, you abandoned the scene of destruction on the tennis court. When the call came through—I had just flown in from Geneva, and both your parents were on the West Coast—I was able to reach the scene minutes before the panicked servants would have cleaned it up. I shot at least a half hour of video before instructing them how to box up separately each of the shattered models and to load the boxes into the back of my car, handling with particular care the little cloth and plastic models of your grandmother and me and of course you and your sister, most of which had been singed and dismembered by the force of the various blasts. I have since had the boxes properly labeled and added to the duplicate collection I keep in the archives, Fabian, along with the video, of which you will come into possession at some future date. In the meantime you will have to live with your much diminished collection of only nine items and its haunting absences. I understand the smears of blackened clay on the tennis court have since been brushed away.

It seems you have still not realized the difference between the models of your collection, which have been painstakingly researched and commissioned by your grandfather, and those other, ordinary models bought at a model shop, which as far as I'm concerned you can blow up or drop rocks on to your heart's content, filling your household industrial-size dumpster to the brim, for all I care.

However, I am not an insensitive ogre. *Boys will be boys*, as I know quite well from my own personal experience. It is clear you are passing through a somewhat late destructive phase in which you take interest and pleasure in breaking things open, blowing them up, seeing when and how they will crack apart and what's inside them—usually nothing, sad to say.

I am fully aware that in a world based on combustion, in a world that worships combustion in all its forms—from the muffled heart-throbbing explosions deep within the internal combustion engine to the televised flashes of smart bombs sent to their targets on the ground from tens of thousands of feet overhead—were we to arrange the world in such a way that boys could no longer be boys, were we to hide all the matches and fireworks, all the guns and bombs, we would soon find ourselves making an about-face and shuffling back toward the Stone Age.

The point being, Fabian, that there is nothing wrong in principle with blowing things up, particularly other people's things. What is wrong is to blow up your own things, or worse, to allow your clever friend Christopher to destroy gifts chosen by your grandfather with great thought and deliberation and no little expense.

By way of a P.S., given that severe headwinds have extended this flight to Brussels by almost an hour. The captain confided to me that in fifteen years of flying he had never experienced headwinds of such force. Be that as it may, last week must have been a national week of vandalism. Only a day after you and your Christopher's tennis court labors, our long-dormant graffiti artist struck down in the Village in the parking lot where I had left the Bentley Azure convertible parked for all of five minutes while I signed some urgent papers in the bank. I returned to find scratched in the metallic blue paint of its hood the following inscription: PrOPErTY IS THEFT. There were the usual police reports, which took an intolerable half an hour, before I was able to drive the car back to the Manor and order my mechanics to completely remove the hood and arrange to have it framed under glass to hang on the wall of the Manor dining room, work which I hope will be completed by the time I return the day after tomorrow.

Future guests will enjoy and be amused by my "artwork." Happily our graffiti artist has miscalculated, leaving his handiwork in a form that could be readily appropriated. PrOPErTY IS THEFT, indeed. Or, as we used to say in my youth, Finders keepers.

Sooner or later one of my guests is bound to offer to pay far more for it than the cost of crating and shipping the replacement by express air freight from England, plus the not inconsiderable cost of the brand new hood itself . . .

And Rowena, lest you think that you can get away with your own little pranks by hiding behind your brother's shame, you will notice that I have locked the glass doors of the cabinet that houses your collection of model cars. I know your distaste for olives, raisins, and anchovies in particular, which your mother fears might be the sign of an eating disorder, which distaste you have prominently displayed by lining the offending objects up in a very straight row on the edge of your dinner plate—until recently, when we all breathed a sigh of relief, thinking that you had changed at last, and that at ten years of age you had finally decided to become a proper young woman. As the only one of the family who periodically inspects your collection, which I have spent so much effort amassing, I happened to open the cabinet door one evening before dinner at your house and was struck by a very peculiar odor emanating from the 1:24 scale Lincoln Town Car Stretch, whose front passenger door you had left open, presumably the last time you crammed the offending morsels inside. I sent the model back to the manufacturers for a proper cleaning, explaining that the household had been invaded by pack rats. The cloth models of your grandmother and me in the back seat were so moldy they had to be replaced.

But this was not entirely why I have not given you driving lessons in the Bentley in our living room, though you may think so. It is true that I cannot feel as keenly about your developing womanhood as I can about Fabian's imminent transformation into a young man, because I know little about girlhood or young womanhood or even fully mature womanhood, except in your case as the future mother of the grandchildren I am unlikely ever to see, except in the form of the trust funds that I have already established for them.

Be that as it may, I have told you repeatedly that you could watch from the back seat, but twice now you have run pouting to your grandmother, which only goes to demonstrate my point. Although I have been meticulous in bestowing exactly identical models on you and your brother for your collections in order to subvert impulses of sibling rivalry, the fact of the matter is that there are great bands of divergence between the sexes, which are bound to become greater and greater with the passage of time—all part of that elaborate training for you and your brother to assume possession of the world of *things*. Girls, if I understand correctly, are trained to assume possession of all that is soft and plump, while boys will be directed toward what is hard and sharp. Not, of course, to exclude either of you from the opposite tastes as an occasional exercise, so much as to suggest that while Fabian learns to "drive" a hard, heavy object of countless kinds of metal and filled with reservoirs of toxic, sticky, greasy, and combustible substances, any one of which, if served up as soup could kill off the lot of us—and I mean here of course gasoline, motor oil, anti-freeze, battery acid, grease, transmission fluid, mineral oil, rear-end oil—what is in short tucked inside a Bentley as well as inside any other automobile—that while Fabian learns to "drive" you should learn how to "ride" in the back seat. There you may enjoy the look and feel of split cowhide, woolen carpet, lambskin carpet overlays, and the finest English veneers. And there you may reflect, if you wish, on the four cattle and four lambs that have been humanely slaughtered for your comfort, on the walnut trees felled, and on the sheep sheared. Most of this work was undoubtedly done by men with sharp implements such as shears, knives, saws, axes, and the like, in their restless endeavors to create a soft plump environment for the women of the world. So by refusing to ride as a passenger in the back seat, Rowena, you may be endangering your future role first as a young woman and second as a fully mature one. I can only hope that your grandmother Deirdre is explaining these facts of industrial life to you as you sit whispering to each other on the sofa while I teach Fabian how to drive, though the cold looks in our direction suggest that she may be propagandizing you with other kinds of thoughts.

The recent abuse of your valuable collections by both of you, Fabian and Rowena, has made me thankful that I have already embarked on assembling that other collection of actual real cars, or their contemporary replacements if we cannot track down and restore the cars I once actually owned. On this flight to Milan, I have been going over the conceptual drawings which illustrate how the cars will be housed in a large showroom in the ninety-acre field immediately to the west of your grandmother's agricultural folly, Martha Washington's Nap Organic Acres. The hundred-car complex of period automobile dealership showrooms and garages—the size will allow future expansion of my collection—will be designed by a world-class architect and will feature complete repair, restoration, and maintenance facilities staffed by dozens of mechanics and restorers. Upon my demise, the collection will be named after me and bestowed on the National Park Service to maintain in perpetuity as a memorial to the wonderfully inventive and generous man I was.

Well, still am.

30. 1:8 SCALE 1997 MERCEDES-BENZ 500SL COUPE

THIS SOMEWHAT SMALLER CAR, WHOSE SILVER PAINT reflected nicely the Barbed Wire Robber Baron's sterling silver tea service, we were able to fit into the dining room by making some simple modifications to the French doors which now look out, unfortunately, onto the organic farm. Their new function as garage doors is not visible even to the trained eye—your grandmother being the one exception.

They're not the same, she claimed over dinner one evening when your father under some feeble pretext canceled your plans to join us. *I can see the difference.*

Of course they're the same. Nothing has been changed. They are identical, exactly the same, twins, you might say, quite unchanged.

Then what about that crack?

What crack?

She seemed to be pointing over the roof of the Mercedes to a crack at the top of the wooden pillar that separated the two banks of French doors, where the pillar had been sawed off in order to allow both banks of French doors, now fastened together, to swing outward like barn doors to allow the car to be rolled or driven in and out of the dining room.

That crack, she said, *was never there before.*

Well it is now, because it allows the doors to open and close in order to admit the Mercedes 500SL, which I find a particularly attractive car.

She was silent a few minutes while chewing on her salad. Then she asked, *Did it belong to Adolph Hitler?*

I dropped my fork. *How could it belong to Hitler when he's been dead fifty-some years? No, of course not, but so what if it did?*

Doesn't it have that swastika-thing on the hood?

That is not a swastika thing. That's a three pointed star.

They all look the same to me, she observed, picking at her salad. *I thought I read somewhere they should have closed all those companies down and banned their swastika-thing brands after the war, where did I read that?*

I wouldn't know, I muttered. *I leave reading to others. It was Henry Ford himself who said "History is bunk." The only history that isn't bunk is the history I'm living right now.*

I knew this would cause her to change the subject. It did.

Do you like the salad? she asked.

Salad's salad, isn't salad just salad, I ask you?

She craned her neck to see around the roof of the Mercedes and then pointed with her fork. *It came from down there, next to those poles.*

It's limp. They need to fly it back and forth across the country a few times to toughen it up.

Your grandmother, I must tell you two, can be a little punitive now and then. The next thing she would tell me, I feared, was that the vegetables down there were grown with composted human waste.

It was grown using composted human waste, she said.

How could I enjoy my first dinner with the Mercedes in the dining room with remarks like that?

31. 1:12 SCALE 1997 ROLLS-ROYCE SILVER SPUR III

THE OCCASION ON WHICH I HAVE CHOSEN TO ADD THIS 1:12 scale 1997 black Rolls-Royce Silver Spur III to your collections is rather trivial: the tenth anniversary of Thingie® Corporation International profits reaching $10 billion a quarter for four consecutive quarters. Trivial, that is, in comparison with the historic event that was to have unfolded only this last week in the form of a visit to Fairlawn-Fairview Lake Manor scheduled by the President of the United States, on the occasion of the big one, which is of course my latest birthday. My contributions to his campaign and the party have been substantial, both personal and through the sixty-eight subsidiaries of Thingie®-Gazillion International. And your contributions too, Fabian and Rowena, as we have employed all seventeen loopholes to the full extent permitted by law, for each and every member of the family, excluding of course your *liberal democrat* father.

What I really wanted and what I got—admittedly two days shy of my actual birthday, owing to the press of corporate and international events—was a ride in the presidential limousine, which probably cost me close to two million dollars in contributions. Every penny was worth it, I assure you. I should enter it in the *Guinness Book of World Records* as the world's most expensive taxi ride ever, from the CIA air base fifteen miles down the road to our front door. I was told to be waiting at the base at exactly 5:17 P.M. for the President to be helicoptered in, whereupon we would ride up to the house, which had been thoroughly inspected the day before. My gun collection was temporarily removed and three cases of exhibition-grade fireworks were uncovered in the garage—about which we will speak soon, Fabian—and we had to send Flora back to Panama for the week and put up with the presidential chef and taster for two days in advance.

But all to no avail, in the end. True, I got my ride, but without the President, whose schedule was revised owing to the West Coast earthquakes. I'm having a 1:12 scale model of the 2000 Cadillac Presidential Limousine commissioned for your collections with removable panels revealing bullet- and bomb-proofing and other security features. It will be the one car in the collections that I have neither owned nor driven but which I include as a memento of this almost historic event. I will only note that the car suffered from a persistently annoying rattle coming from somewhere inside the headliner above my head.

The model will be fitted with 1:12 scale models of me and the President sitting in the back seat. For those spoilsports who may complain of the historical inaccuracy of this scene, I can only suggest that a slight discrepancy lies not in our sitting in the back seat of the limousine, for we have both sat there, but only in sitting there simultaneously, which in time will come to seem quite the quibble.

32. 1:12 SCALE 1998 HUMMER H-1

AS I COMPOSE THESE WORDS ON MY WAY TO SÃO Paulo—a quick trip before my big one—I cannot help but still see you two, Fabian and Rowena, standing before me when you were perhaps five and three, rapt with wonder at whatever little speech I was giving to you, almost a whole decade ago—eyes wide, mouths agape, in your fuzzy bunny-suit pajamas—perhaps on the occasion of my presenting you with the very first models of your collection. Who would have guessed you might so soon become almost unrecognizable adolescents from outer space? Fortunately your good Delahunt teeth, Fabian, will need no straightening and you will be spared having your mouth turned into the major construction zone that Rowena's has become.

Be that as it may, as a captain of industry myself—though I consider that ranking now to be far too low—a five-star general of industry would be more like it—I will be expected to make a few remarks on the actual occasion of the big one, apropos of my long and successful life, and how I have witnessed the march of progress going faster and faster, from a walk and then a jog, to a race and then a dash or sprint, churning out ever greater quantities of spin-off products on the way, to the benefit of that portion of mankind who can afford these items or obtain the necessary credit for their purchase, lease, or rental. My addition to your collections of the 1:12 scale 1998 Hummer H-1, whose early history I would frankly rather forget, is not to mark that occasion, however, which is still ahead of us, but is rather to celebrate the failure of the Hamburger Flipper Union to unionize the Gazillion branch of Thingie®-Gazillion International. They need to change their name, incidentally, now that all hamburgers are flipped abroad and only warmed within the contiguous forty-eight.

Be that as it may, my remarks will be about the wheel. How the wheel has done it all. I cannot claim to have invented the wheel, much as I would have liked to. And even tried to. Think of the returns on a patent on that one. My lawyers have been researching it for more than twenty years and have recently outlined a case to argue that nineteen patents I have submitted for the wheel were unfairly and illegally rejected by the U. S. Patent Office.

Be that as it may, much of mankind's engineering effort has been in attempting to convert reciprocal action, which is the tiresome pumping up and down of legs while walking, for example, into smooth linear movement across rough and bumpy land. The first wheels achieved that remarkable end without notably increasing speed. The advent of the steam and internal combustion engine re-introduced the reciprocating action of legs and sexual organs and through various systems involving flywheels, clutches, and gears converted such action into circular rolling movement, with wheels.

Now it's all very well to go *so what?* and *ho-hum* at this point and fail to notice the important action of the geometric proliferation of the wheel throughout the world, in the way it has smoothed, compacted, abraded, pounded down, firmed up, buffed, and polished the earth, and in general how the wheel has been such a dynamic force in rendering so much of the surface of the earth ever smoother and therefore ever more friendly and hospitable to the wheel. It is the wheel that draws forth more asphalt, more cement, more gravel in ever greater quantities over ever increasing surfaces of land. *Pave me*, the world cries out before the wheel, *pave me over. Let there be rivers of pavement, fields of pavement, lakes of pavement, seas of pavement, oceans and oceans of pavement; let us dream of paving until the very end of time.*

The ever-restless wheel seeks out ever more opportunities as we rush to build machines to satisfy its craving to smooth the rough, flatten the corrugated, round off the edges of nature: the roller skate, the mountain bike, the skateboard, the ATV, the SUV, all clearing deserts of brush, forests of trees, jungles of whatever they are cleared of, plus the great wheels of jet airliners with their unquenchable thirst for entire square miles of thick reinforced concrete. Where once it was the sword, the spear, the crossbow, the musket, the rifle, the cannon, smallpox, the mortar, the tank, the atom bomb, napalm, and Agent Orange that subdued the earth, now it is simply and elegantly the wheel, in the form of those countless tires upon which we ride each day, knowing each time we step into a car and sit down that we will experience a quiet moment of joy sent up our spine by the first instants of rolling.

The wheel, to which all shoulders are now applied, rich and poor, *Conservative Republican* and *liberal democrat* alike, the wheel, which all labor for and worship, from the child going *rrrn-rrrn* as he pushes the small metal toy car back and forth on the carpet, to the elder five-star general of industry, who with the push of a button can cause millions of wheels to start turning all over the world. And in the middle of a seventy-mile-an-hour bumper-to-bumper rush hour on a ten-lane interstate, who of you has not been amazed at the thrumming whine of hundreds of rapidly turning tires and the little gasps they make as they hit seams and cracks in the pavement?

The wheel: human evolution will have reached its pinnacle when the earth is finally paved over, and nature is confined to a few large estates and carefully managed reserves which we will visit on Sundays, the reserves not the estates, and ride about in them on monorails and hovercraft with our grandchildren—if we can tear them away from their own myriad wheeled conveyances.

Unfortunately I will not be alive for that great event, the final paving over, which is estimated to take place at 6:39 P.M. Eastern Daylight Time, August 21, 2076, and therefore I will be unable to join in the massive global celebrations to be organized around it—unless the new freeze-dry cloning technique responds well to a recent infusion of capital. In any case, to all those who will be there, I convey my very best wishes for a wonderful event. If unable to be there in body, I will certainly be there in spirit.

Such will be the substance of my speech. I will not of course reveal to the assembled throng the final preparations I have begun to sketch out, for the black and chrome semi tractor trailer hearse, on whose flatbed will be borne my favorite car festooned with black bunting, with my suitably stabilized earthly remains firmly positioned behind the wheel, tactfully shaded by my favorite hat and dark glasses. My ultimate destination will be a simple limestone mausoleum built in the form of a two-car garage, the other slot being reserved for your grandmother and her favorite car, and into which the car, with me in it, will be gently rolled. At that moment, the stone garage "door" will rise up from the earth on hydraulic cylinders to seal me within, forever and ever—or until the perfection of the freeze-dried cloning technique, which has begun to show promise with salamanders.

And other such thoughts—or rather, thoughts more suitable to a joyous public occasion, I will deliver from the south portico of the Manor, to the assembled Thingie®-Gazillion International upper and middle management and spouses on the occasion of my next big one in exactly five days, predicted to be a clear and crisp autumn day, with temperatures in the low seventies, and the first maple leaves beginning to turn.

33. 1:8 SCALE 2000 LAMBORGHINI DIABLO VT

THIS, MY DEAR FABIAN, IS THE CAR YOU WILL ACTUALLY learn to drive on—if I have anything to do with it. Which I may or may not, given the reception your father greeted the presentation of this mere model with you, at 1:8 scale, behind the wheel. They are getting better at this, though your wardrobe for the car seems a little odd: some rakish double-breasted Italian leather sports coat, it looks like, and me in the passenger seat in my blue blazer and a yachting cap. I must talk to them about these details.

I would rather my son learn to drive on a bulldozer than an overpowered Italian muscle car, your father announced after you two had been excused from the table. Our first family dinner together in seven months was not coming to a happy conclusion.

That can be arranged, I suggested. *I'm sure Fabian would love to take a D-9 to the neighborhood.*

Chip turned around in his seat and stared through the archway into the living room, where the real full-size flaming red Lamborghini sat under floodlights. The doors were open and you two, Fabian and Rowena, were sitting inside it and you, Fabian, were gesticulating wildly.

No kid, Chip said, waving his dessert fork, *has ever learned how to drive in a car like that. Not to speak of the fact that I am the one who decides when and how and where and in what my children learn to drive.*

Deedums correctly added, *You decide, and I decide, Chip. We decide.* She re-arranged her napkin. *But the fact is, Chip, neither of us can take the time to give the boy the driving lessons he needs. Therefore their grandfather's offer—*

No.

We went over your court calendar last night, Chip, she continued.

And Chippo, I joined in, *you have to admit that you haven't even found the time to go through the mountain of material I prepared for you and Deedums concerning the purchase of Fabian's first car.*

He threw up his hands. *I intend to ask the boy simply what he wants.*

Well, then that's settled. He confided to me he wanted a flaming red Lamborghini Diablo VT. Unless you were going to ask the poor boy what he wants and then tell him that what he's actually going to get is a dull red Toyota Corolla.

Is that the one he wants? he tossed his head toward the offending car.

No, I corrected, *that one is mine. Upon the successful completion of his driving test, I'll get him his own. He may want another color by then.*

Deirdre, your thoughtful grandmother, chimed in at this point. *I don't see what the problem is. The boy should have what he wants. Bright red is a very visible color. It should be quite safe.*

The discussion ended inconclusively when Chip's cell phone went off and he had to leave the table for a half hour, during which time we adjourned to the living room for coffee and brandy, while you kids sat contentedly in the Lamborghini opening and closing doors and the hood and turning on and off the lights and sound system. With Chip still absent on the phone over an upcoming Supreme Court case, it was a rare moment of family harmony during which it appeared to have been decided that I indeed would be the one to give you, Fabian, your first driving lessons in the Lamborghini as soon as you obtain your learner's permit next month.

This of course is an absolutely crucial moment in the development of the character of any young man, the moment of learning to drive and assuming possession of your very first automobile ever. What you will learn, Fabian, is that first of all you *are* your car—not only in your own mind, through the sleepless imaginings you will suffer night after night as you yearn for the moment of consummation in first possessing it as yours and yours only, but then, again and again, throughout the days and weeks and years when you set forth to find it again in the garage or the parking lot or wait for it to be returned to your hands by the parking valet or the mechanic or the car washing attendant. I hope, in this connection, you will never have to search it out in the impoundment lot.

You are your car not only in terms of your own insatiable longings, for in this at least it is socially permitted and indeed encouraged that you acquire a virtual harem of cars, but also in terms of how people look at you. They will see you as not just you, but as Fabian of the flaming red Lamborghini or of the Bentley or of the Hummer or of the Harley—or of all of the above, and more. Your car announces and proclaims your level of testosterone, your ambitions, your sexual orientation, your age, your economic status, your political orientation, and much more. You probably do not know how fortunate you are in not having to work your way up through a succession of sad little Nissans, cheap Fords, flabby Dodges or Buicks, cars which no doubt wreak havoc on their owners' self-images by painting them as losers, oddballs, marginals, misfits, and malcontents—though in another way we must be thankful for those traffic jams of plain-jane ordinary cars, for setting off our far more magnificent machines. If no one or nothing were ugly, the beautiful would be commonplace—and quite worthless. In driving the cars of the gods, we set off sparks of envy in the eyes of those we sweep past.

What your first car, and especially this one, will offer like no others that come afterward, is the promise to be first, to win the race, to reach the summit, by simply pushing a few pedals and moving a lever or two, pressing some buttons, by an almost effortless labor. In this capsule on wheels, you are offered the promise of achieving all of your hopes and dreams, each and every day you slip body and soul behind its wheel—and all with little effort, almost no thought and hardly any planning, and no discipline other than submitting more or less to the so-called rules of the road. To drive a car: this will be your first great achievement, Fabian.

Yet your eventual success—as revolutionizing engineer, a Titan of investment, a great attorney, whatever—will enable you to see the illusion at the heart of even your most fervent desires, and make you wonder at how something that seems to promise so much, the climbing into your new Lamborghini or some other splendid car, can so often seem to deliver little more than a somewhat weary memory of the road and the traffic and the tiny imperfections of design or finish or handling or performance that seem to plague any car, even the finest and most expensive, or I sometimes think, especially those. Bumper-to-bumper traffic comes to seem an exercise in mass hysteria in which millions and billions of motorists believe they are heading down the road to success when the reality is that they are probably going nowhere fast, like hamsters on a treadmill, and only wearing ruts into a stultifyingly familiar route, and spending themselves eventually into penury to do so, although to the profit of those of us who have invested wisely. Such thoughts often pass through my mind while flying over some metropolitan sprawl at rush hour, in the dark, during winter, and I stare down at the slow-moving rivers of red tail-lights and white headlamps—as I did only forty-five minutes ago after taking off for Brussels.

So, who knows, Fabian, whether you will simply drive your life away, ever hopeful, or whether you will now and then stop and apply yourself to some matter or study or discipline and do the hardest thing—which is to ignore the siren call of these strange creatures we have perfected and which offer, so easily, to spirit us away into a kind of forgetfulness.

But then these *liberal democrat* moments—the media are subtle in their poisons—I snap out of usually in a matter of seconds, and all seems right again. *Go for it Fabian*, I think, *and drive your head off. Don't listen to their moans of envy and spite. Pump that gas. Press that pedal. Fasten your seat belt. And make it the ride of your life.*

While searching for your mother, Fabian, regarding some last minute preparations for my birthday, I popped into your room to make certain there were no more depredations to your collection, much diminished as it was by the tennis court massacre of some time ago now. I had surmised that all was well and I was about to turn away from the display case when I noted a certain fuzziness about the models, my first thought being that my glasses needed cleaning. However, the fuzziness persisted through cleaned glasses. I approached closer and opened the glass doors and reached in and picked up the models one after another and felt a frisson of anger zip up and down my thighs: these were not the carefully handcrafted models I had so painstakingly collected for you at a cost of tens of thousands of dollars, with their opening doors and hoods and trunks and convertible tops, lights that switched on, and little manikins of your grandmother and me and you and Rowena within. These were cheap plastic models mass produced by the millions in Honduras or somewhere and outrageously marked up, and quite hollow inside, light as a feather. My thoughts, as you can imagine, spun round and round.

The housekeeper told me she thought you were down at the pool with *that Christopher friend* and a couple of other boys—all probably, like that Christopher, from dot-com trash families that have begun to infest your end of Fairlawn-Fairview Lake Estates. The bright sunny air cleared my thoughts as I strode down the flagstone path toward the pool, concealed behind a maze of stone walls, hedges, and fences. It was becoming clear that a fake collection had supplanted your real one because of some deal with that Christopher of yours—that very likely he was serving as your fence in order for you to be able to cash in on your collection in order to buy something, but what? Drugs? Not likely, given the frequency with which the dog-sniffing service your parents subscribe to visits the house and most of the neighborhood under that new federal program. I do not approve of your father's insistence of keeping your allowance deliberately low to encourage you to seek other sources of income—which clearly you have begun to do, in engineering a hostile takeover of your collection by another. Is nothing sacred anymore? The answer came soon enough.

I have never understood your parents' desire to enclose their swimming pool at the center of a maze, albeit a light-duty one easily penetrated after the first false steps into dead ends. I quickly arrived at the last hedge, a gap in which presented me with a startling view of a fully mature young man diving naked off the board into the pool—and who I only realized after he had surfaced and scrambled up on to the tile was your friend Christopher. I will not describe the condition of his penis as he bent over and

picked up a bottle of beer and threw his head back and guzzled the contents and then threw it into the hedge on the opposite side of the pool, bursting into a shouted, off-tune rendition of *My girl has ginger hair underneath her underwear.*
. . . You, Fabian, then sailed off the board in a similar condition followed by two other boys equally inflamed, the last with a lit cigarette between his teeth as he plunged beneath the water. This then led to a parade of divings off the board with flowers and other forms of vegetation tucked between stiffly held-together legs, vegetation inserted fore and aft, poorly concealing the condition you were all in. Paralyzed to find myself in this situation, I could not immediately decide whether to withdraw and have it out with you later, Fabian, or step out on to the tile and confront you all. In my state of mind, I was unable to recall the other verses to the song which you had all obviously learned very well. But when an empty beer bottle clipped my ear and smashed on the flagstone behind me—a gleeful *Ooops* came from over the hedge—I realized I had to act.

I stepped forcefully out on to the blue tile apron at the shallow end of the pool, where a skinny gangly kid paddled, watching agog, but with his trunks still on, possibly the Supreme Court Justice's grandson who lives down by the lake. Except for an area immediately below the diving board, the pool was filled with every object the four or five of you were able to shove or toss into the water from the cabana and dressing rooms—tables, the grill, towels, clothing, loungers, chairs, their cushions bobbing on the surface.

Fabian, I bellowed, *attire yourself at once!*

Everyone froze. Erections immediately flagged as towels and swimming trunks were scrambled for.

A tire?

Put on some clothes or something. Put on your trunks. Put on your shirt. Put on a towel, for all I care. But put something on. And come here.

Dripping, you thrust your feet into the leg holes of your maroon trunks and padded over to me, splashing through a thin film of water on the tile. I confess to having to admit to myself that indeed you were now probably slightly taller than I was, as your mother has repeatedly tried to point out to me. You stared at me with a calm blue-eyed insolence, your large teeth gleaming malevolently, as if to say, what was I doing here trying to spoil a moment of—*boys being boys?*

And you, I pointed at the Christopher fellow. He already had chest hair. He already had muscles. A minute ago they were all kids. Overnight they had become vicious gangsters. *And you, clean up the broken glass over there. And everyone else. Every last sliver. And you,* I pointed to another one, *get all that crap out of the pool.* Then I faced you. *And you, Fabian, I'll talk to you later.*

Though it turned out that we never did have that talk, as I suspect you blamed me for getting in trouble with your parents—*But we were going to clean it all up,* being the limp excuse reported to me afterward—and because I became embroiled in negotiating through my lawyers with your Christopher's parents to return the remains of your valuable collection. They claimed it was strictly a business matter between their disreputable son and you, Fabian, with you apparently refusing to return the petty sums of money you were willing to accept for your priceless collection, along with the worse-than-useless cheap models intended to lull me into thinking all was well within your display case.

The remedy is, of course, simple but severe. With one more model, your collection would have been brought up to date, a model I intended to give you on the occasion of my big one. With a stroke of the pen—or with 134 strokes of the pen, to be exact—I have removed you from the rolls of the world's wealthiest individuals, which you may not notice for a while—and which could eventually be repaired, should you finally ever mature into a sober young man respectful of your elders and solicitous of their needs and demands and having assumed a political persuasion compatible with substantial wealth.

You are now, it is clear, leaving the luminous rooms of your childhood and entering the dark ages of adolescence and youth, for which I will presume to offer, even if with a sense of futility, a piece of advice. By now your Christopher has surely proven how unreliable and dangerous friends can be, how they can lead you astray, fleece you of what you should value, and so on. My advice is simple. Make *things* your friends. *Things* will never let you down, they will not betray you or take advantage of you, they will not envy you, and conveniently, you can dispose of them at a moment's notice, without excuse or guilt, trading them in on newer and better models, of which there will always be a great abundance.

All I can do now is to wish you the best of luck, in the fond hope that when you finally emerge from this dark age—if you do emerge, for many don't—as a responsible young man, that you and I will now and then be able to sit down after dinner, swirling our brandies next to the fireplace, and reminisce about the old days, and even laugh about them. I do look forward to those moments and in particular to inquiring discreetly if you might still happen to remember the rest of the verses to that delightful old song, *My Girl Has Ginger Hair*. It has taken me weeks to get the damned thing out of my mind.

But I jump ahead of the day. The worst was yet to come. In some ways. I was unable to complete the account on my night flight to Cape Town due to a flurry of calls but I hope there will be time to do so on this return trip.

To resume, I had no sooner settled myself in behind the inlaid walnut steering wheel of my brand new Bentley Azure convertible parked in front of your house, Fabian and Rowena, a pre-birthday present to myself, and was sinking into its soft leather seat—just getting inside that car and inhaling the fragrance of wool, wood, and leather makes everything else entirely worth it, the constant pushing, the endless legal skirmishing, the poring over the numbers again and again and again, the 3:00 A.M. wrestlings with the next mergers or the next de-acquisitions, the damned restlessness of it all—and I was struck as if by lightning by the awful thought, *I'll bet the rascals have got her collection too.* I immediately shut off the ignition and let the automatic seat and steering wheel de-position themselves to let me out and then I strode across the lawn and in through the front door where the housekeeper told me she thought you, Rowena, were still out with your mother down at the village. So I proceeded straight upstairs to your room and pushed open the door and planted myself in front of the glass case which houses your collection and almost fainted when I detected the same fuzziness hovering about your models. Quickly I picked them up one by one and flipped them over. All empty, cheap imported plastic imitations, some not even the right year and model. The scoundrels had indeed got away with the lot. I was devastated.

I can't believe you were complicit in this fraud, Rowena, but even if not I am astounded that you let your valuable collection be spirited away probably one item at a time, without noticing that something was wrong, probably not even noticing that the case was unlocked, its lock probably picked by that Christopher kid.

You can imagine the mood I was in when I slipped from your room, not improved by the sound of belching coming from the half open door to your brother's room across the hall, his sopping wet trunks left in the middle of the carpet. So much for the long-planned driving lessons and the purchase of his first car, not that there had been much doubt for the last hour or so. I went downstairs and returned to the Bentley where I sat for a good fifteen minutes without starting it, reflecting on the fragility of all our hopes for the next generation, who seem unable to accept our gifts, indeed all our wealth and treasure, or to perform even the most perfunctory displays of gratitude. Thank god, I thought, at least I still have myself to thank for all I have helped bring into the world. For the myriad *things* I have created out of almost nothing. For the financial Everest heaped up out of all those one-hundredths of a cent. Thank you, I said to myself, thank you.

But even this glowing moment was to come to an end when for the first time in years—such has been the pace— I was visited by images of my simple, unambitious parents and their little house, so sparsely furnished, on a tree-lined street where their few friends seemed larger and more life-size and dramatic than today's pygmies. They still lived in a world where nothing was automatic, nothing powered, where the work of us engineers was mainly to design things to run a little longer and prevent them from burning up or flying apart. And in a time when all the world was left to desire, long before things changed and we ended up having everything, with nothing left to want, nothing lacking, and hundreds, indeed thousands of people waiting to carry out my every whim. But what happens when you don't have any more whims? When you are whimless? Whimmed out? Perhaps this is something like the *simple life* your grandmother Deirdre endlessly hankers for, a life like an old black-and-white movie with a tent and an old car and an aluminum teakettle perched on blackened rocks over a smoky flame, and men and women wearing stained gray cotton clothing and having earnest discussions about money, while the kids play tag in the trees.

You don't talk to me anymore, Deirdre, I finally said to her the other night after our twentieth silent dinner. I have been in the air 146 times already this year and thought it time to settle down for a few days.

What is there to talk about? she said with unusual severity. She has become an amazingly handsome old thing, finally sure of herself, even behind the wheel. *We have everything we have ever needed or wanted. Our daughter is successful beyond all imagining, needs nothing.We have turned our grandchildren into spoiled, envious brats.You look down on everyone who has less than we do, which encompasses the entire world.We will live forever, our doctors successfully beating back disease after disease. So what is there to talk about?*

In my theory of Industrial Sex, marriage is like a well-oiled and well-maintained internal combustion engine. Quarrels and quibbles and so-called misunderstandings are signs that the oil needs changing or some component is wearing out, a bearing or a bushing, and that in general the vastly complicated mechanism designed to control *combustion*, which is to say to keep *combustion* internal to the machine, is showing the first signs of breaking apart and spilling out inflammable substances toward open sparks. Poor maintenance inevitably leads to divorce. Our marriage clearly needed a major overhaul. I suggested a quick trip around the world—Hawaii, Bali, Thailand, South Africa, Paris, and so on—in our own 767. A truly carefree holiday. Just the two of us. Plus of course crew, translators, guides, a driver. And I almost forgot, a chef.

No, she said, looking away.Then she turned to me with

a half-smile. *But why don't you come down to the shelter tomorrow over in Hartford where I'm on night duty?*

I'll take a rain check, thank you, I muttered, briefly afflicted with a hellish vision of row upon row of army cots sagging under the weight of their raggedly clothed occupants—and not bothering to explain it was out of the question because I had phone calls and teleconferences scheduled for the next forty-eight hours because of some nonsense in our Asian divisions about currency instabilities.

The irrelevant recollections faded and I was about to start the car when out of the bushes about a hundred yards away, from the north side of the maze surrounding the pool, three boys emerged running and throwing things and snapping their towels at each other, essentially naked, and shouting and laughing, trailed after by the gangly, bony boy who was at least decently attired in his swimming trunks. They were all headed across the grass toward the gatehouse. Then, a minute later, four girls in bikinis slipped out from the hedge not far from where I had been standing. They sauntered over to the house, holding their untied halters, such as they were, to their budding young breasts. I finally realized one of them was you, Rowena, head thrown back and laughing with the others and bumping and butting up against each other as you disappeared inside the house.

As soon as the boys had passed the gatehouse, each throwing something inside the door at, I gather, the security guard—popping sounds soon confirmed that the somethings were fire crackers and cherry bombs—and disappearing into the woods, I started the Bentley and slowly drove away, heading down the drive toward the smoke-filled gate-house—the guard was standing outside trying to fan the smoke outside—deeply bewildered and saddened by the realization that your days of collecting fine precision model cars were, apparently, very much over.

Yet, after all the dust has settled, it has occurred to me that you two, Fabian and Rowena, have reached the age at which you might appreciate the insights of my *General Theory of Industrial Sex.* I would in fact present both of you with copies of a leather-bound edition but for the fact that your father has been dropping hints to the effect that my visits to the house have become too frequent for his taste and, more explicitly, would I please *call ahead.* I, who never *call ahead.* I, who have based a whole revolutionary management system on *never calling ahead* as laid out in complete detail in my best-selling *The Never-Call-Ahead Management Technique: How to Convert Your Business to the "Surprise Visit" System and Triple Productivity and Profits in Ten Easy Steps.* Probably so I won't stumble on yet another of their interminable quarrels.

So that event will have to wait until somewhat later when I present you both with copies of this commentary to your model car collections—even though it's fair to say that your collections no longer exist in any meaningful form, and this tome, which you will eventually hold in your hands, will be quite pointless without them. Or less meaningful. Christopher Burr's parents have refused entry into their house by either me or my representatives—I find it hard to believe that their own connection with the upper echelon of the FBI could possibly trump my own, but there it is. Sweeps of Eastern Seaboard pawnshops and model shows have failed to recover a single model, leading me to believe that your Christopher is now the serious collector among your set, and that each night as he goes to bed he gazes fondly at an illuminated case which probably houses the forty-three surviving exemplars of your two collections.

Learning to drive, which is really a matter of learning how to control internal combustion engines, is the first and only formal lesson in sex you will probably every have. I regret that circumstances of your creating have forced me to withdraw my offer to teach you how to drive. I also seriously doubt you will be able to truly appreciate my various volumes, including this one, until you are well into your thirties if not forties. Be that as it may, after whatever lessons you do get, you are on your own. When boys, who eventually become men, tell jokes of a certain kind, they are really thinking about cars; and when they're working on their cars, they're really thinking about sex. This is at the core of my General Theory. This simple lesson I learned not from the words but from the actions of my own father, who kept car magazines in his bedroom and tacked photos from girlie magazines above his workbench in the garage.

Now women have their own form of internal combustion, which I don't pretend to understand. In fact I see the internal combustion engine as being far more male than female. This is regarded as a fault, no doubt, in these times, but there it is. As a consequence, I find it easier to imagine the female parts as being represented by the path, the driveway, the road, the interstate highway, down which the male drives his internal-combustion-powered projectile or vehicle.

The *glandular* basis of my General Theory also explains why the private automobile has won out over other forms of transportation and why it will continue to dominate the world, assuredly forever—traffic itself being the frenzied commingling of our collective testosterone and estrogen, in a non-stop orgasm of our never-stop age.

But perhaps I go too far for minds still somewhat tender and unopened to the infinite ramifications of my General Theory, the truths of which life is bound to reveal to you in a far more disordered and painful way.

34. 1:8 SCALE 2000 BENTLEY AZURE CONVERTIBLE

THIS WAS TO HAVE BEEN THE LAST SCALE MODEL CAR IN your collection, Fabian and Rowena, bringing us up to date, with the possibility of an addendum collection to be added incrementally as I acquire the last ten or twenty cars of my life—or more, if I decide to become a serious collector of classic cars. I am discussing this possibility with my architects. The 1:8 scale model of the 2000 metallic blue Bentley Azure—with passable 1:8 scale models of you, Fabian, dressed in T-shirt and shorts behind the wheel, me in sport coat and driving hat and gloves sitting next to you and pointing at something ahead in the road as I give you the driving lesson which in fact will never take place, and you, Rowena, in tennis whites in the back seat—took almost as long as the actual car to manufacture. The Azure itself is a special order-car which needs eight months to construct, plus two months to incorporate my custom features. I ordered the scale models for your collections at the same time, well before I realized you had chosen in fact to liquidate them. These models will go to the duplicate collections to be housed in the future Leon Tuggs Museum of Personal Transportation, with one to be held back and placed with the rest of the set in the trunk of my favorite car in which I will be installed or mounted behind the wheel following my death and relevant preservation measures, including twenty-four-hour video surveillance to discourage the sort of looting that so plagued the Egyptians. At this point, early I hope, I still agonize over which is or was or might eventually be my favorite car, but I trust I will be able to make the decision in time.

I have tried on various occasions to bring up this delicate matter with your grandmother, offering her two choices, which are that she can either have herself preserved and mounted in the front seat next to me in my favorite car or else she can choose a car of her own to be parked next to mine in the "garage." After several tries I was at last success-ful over dinner last Sunday night. At least in gaining her attention.

I trust you have seen, I said, waving my hand in general direction past the Lamborghini, *and perhaps even taken some passing interest in the new construction, to the west of my personal automobile museum site.*

What?

You could not have failed to notice on the way down to the organic farm the radiant white stone walls. The stone comes from the same quarry as the Washington Monument.

Oh that, she said with a sigh. *It looks like a garage. A marble garage. Why would you want to build a garage out of white marble?*

In fact that's exactly what it is, an exact replica of my parents' detached two-car garage. The only place in my childhood where I was truly happy, gazing at the centerfolds above my father's narrow masonite-covered workbench and now and then pushing aside the old playing cards he had tacked in front of their erogenous zones.

It's a special kind of garage, I attempted to explain, *a sort of permanent garage. A garage for all time. A final parking place of a garage.*

I will not be buried in a garage, she muttered.

This is no ordinary garage, I said, firing up some enthusiasm even though I knew she had probably already made up her mind in advance. *This is a reinforced concrete garage with special structural features that will guarantee that when the concrete door finally closes, it will close for all time. Instead of pivoting down from the ceiling, you see, it rises up from the ground on hydraulic cylinders which then swivel and lock into place. It's my own patented design. My eighth patent, as a matter of fact.*

With us inside. Or you, rather.

With our remains inside.

She looked up at me at last with a startled expression. *Like mummies?*

What else do you want to be? I for one have always admired the way the Egyptians dragged as much of the stuff of their daily lives as they could into their tombs. The thought of sitting behind the wheel of my favorite car for all eternity was far from an unpleasant thought. In fact, I rather look forward to the experience, as it were.

I want to be composted.

Well, I said, trying to think that one through as fast as I could. *Then you go get yourself composted, at the appropriate time, of course, and then have yourself put in a box, which can rest on the front seat beside me.*

You have missed the point as usual. I want to re-enter the cycle of living and dying to see if I can't do much better next time.

So once again we reached the point of the irreconcilable, she wanting to become worms and voles, and me wanting to realize that ultimate ambition of mankind, to become a *thing*, to become locked or frozen or dried into *thingdom*, for all time.

Your grandmother, it is fair to say, has never learned to appreciate the value of *ego*, surely one of the great inventions of the human spirit. At an early age I learned that if a large ego was a useful tool then an even larger ego was even more effective—and that having once made the discovery that a tack hammer is just fine for tacks but will not do if you want to hammer together a whole house, for which you need a framing hammer. At any rate, I have never looked back. Before a good ripe and fully developed ego, all obstacles fall. I am never wrong about anything, of course. But when the perception of others is that I am wrong or very wrong, it is my ego that comes to my rescue and assures me that deep down I am both right and know I am right. More often than not an apparently wrong decision is a feint on the road to success, in order to flush my enemies out into the open and put my friends to the test. The large ego wastes nothing. Even fine and imprisonment can be excellent ego-building exercises as long as you have salted enough resources away in safe places. Only poverty can be said to bring the bullmoose ego finally down to its knees. An ego that has no *things* with which to trumpet its taste or its boldness or its limitless cravings is nothing but an empty mask.

With my many things and properties and investments and corporations and cars my monumental ego will face death without fear or loneliness. It will stride up to the moment in cocky disbelief, because it knows itself to be always the one exception, often the one and only exception, the one who will get away with something, since it has always managed to get away with virtually everything. And even if this is all an illusion, which of course I also know it to be, my ego will barge on through the one-way swinging doors quite as if this is some minor bureaucratic or medical misunderstanding that will be as usual settled by threats of litigation or transfer or termination or bribes of promotion. I will advance into the void clutching the hand of my ego, secure in the belief that this cannot happen, is not happening, will never happen, up to the very last instant, because these are the words with which my ego, my wonderfully strong and confident and defiant ego, have always whispered to me, especially in the darkest of moments.

But some last advice, my Fabian and Rowena, since the subject seems to be impinging on everyone, with the approach of my next big one, the day after tomorrow, after months of preparation. With the passing of a little more time, I plan to pull my ego aside and have a long heart-to-heart talk with it during which I will strongly advocate the lifting of my impulsive disinheriting of the both of you. I can guarantee no success here, and even if it does go through with its unfortunate egotistical little plans, you will still through your parents and grandmother be able to count yourself among the top five percentile, even after those criminal death taxes. What you need to remember is that when you come into your inheritance, whether large or mammoth, you will be giving purpose to thousands and even millions of lives, and that you will have succeeded in subverting the squalid *liberal democrat* urges of the age—and of your father—and have become secretly a king and a queen in an era which likes to think itself above such things. The mass of humankind, my pets, will always need its kings and queens, call them what they will. If we have chosen to disguise ourselves, it is because we now wisely fear the people's guillotines, its show trials, its media frenzies, its taste for stripping us naked and herding us through the streets like cattle and sheep—as they have been known to do in certain benighted countries of the world. We have successfully turned money into a finely penetrating solvent that can escape through the tiniest orifices and cracks to seek deeper, quieter, and safer chambers, gated communities within gated communities within gated communities.

What they don't know, yet crave to know, is how very ordinary we might be, which is why we must conceal ourselves behind our treasured things, behind the walls of our vast mansions, the tinted glass of our opulent cars, the rare materials of our clothing, until we can believe, through our things, led by our egos, that we too are indeed rare and precious beings, unlike any others that have ever walked—or driven across—the face of the earth.

Yet when all is said and done, little King Fabian, little Queen Rowena, the soul is forever restless, even so—and especially when you think that you possess at last everything you have ever dreamed of.

Therefore prepare, my young ones. Prepare for the worst.

ADDENDUM A:
1934 DUESENBERG DUAL COWL
PHAETON, BODY BY DIETRICH

I WAS OF COURSE PLEASED TO SEE YOU, FABIAN AND Rowena, if only from a distance, at the gala celebration of my big one, for which I arrived behind the wheel of the 1934 Duesenberg Dietrich Dual Cowl Phaeton, with the top down, a little present to myself—at least before it moves into the new annex of the Leon Tuggs Museum of Personal Transportation which will house two hundred of the world's best cars, once I acquire them. I don't know that I would have wanted to examine your flaming orange hair, Fabian, up close. The Duesenberg is the first of the new collection. Despite some battery trouble, my arrival at the south portico via some specially laid down paving material to prevent the grass from being damaged—my arrival corresponded exactly, as planned, to the moment when thousands of miniature Gazillion Burgers were released from a transport circling overhead, for the delectation of nearly three thousand middle- and upper-management guests, plus spouses. The mini-burgers wafted down on little parachutes promoting our latest line of *Lobster Lickers,* whose 1.7 percent

real lobster content we are allowed to list as the principal
ingredient since a recent loosing up of restrictive labeling
regulations brought about by a vigorous and inventive lob-
bying campaign. I'm sure when your mother Deedums wins
her election to the Senate, as she obviously will, she'll
improve the legislation even more. They were all snapped
up, out of the air, and even off the ground, as per my memo
suggesting that anyone who did not join in the fun and games
would be summarily fired. Except of course for several hundred mini-burgers which, owning to a change in the wind,
came to land in the fields and on top of the greenhouses of
Martha Washington's Nap Organic Farm, which led to your
grandmother taking me to court under the charge of being
the source of a drift onto her organic fields of *illegal pesticides
or herbicides or other substances not approved for organic produc-
tion*, to quote the silly language of the suit. Apparently,
Rowena, you have taken to working down there on weekends soaking up the beneficial aromas of manure—*nostalgie
de la boue* is a hard one to stamp out—and I would appreciate it if you could somehow indicate to me the real extent of
the damages to your grandmother's precious lettuces and
arugula. Minimal, I suspect. And mostly, I also suspect, from
crazed inmates of the farm running across the beds trying to
catch one of the Gazillion Burgers while still airborne and
then flattening themselves on the ground to gobble it down,
starving vegetarians as they are, before they could be caught
by the farm's *diet police*.

Otherwise the event was an astounding success. I
delivered my birthday address, a celebration of the wheel,

from the south portico of the Manor to the collective management of all my corporations. Commemorative collector packets of Thingies® were handed out on silver platters, and the event ended with an evening fireworks display over the lake, which added to the litigation mentioned above.

Your grandmother was not present, as I had expected. For some time I have reconciled myself to the existence of that desert that yawns in time between man and wife, a place littered with the skeletons of indiscretion and infidelity— mine mostly, I gather. An arid, silent place where the slightest word or belch or yawn is an announcement that there will be no relief from hostilities, on the rare evening she shows up at the Manor on the way out of town from seeing Deedums and you two and when she occasionally consents to sit down at the dinner table.

I find I am spending more time in the air than ever— these words are being scribbled on my way to Warsaw—and landing is always a great sadness. Given recent events, I have decided it might be wiser to withhold these reflections until you are grandparents yourselves and when you both will be of an age to appreciate my seasoned and candid view of your errant youths, or at least those small slivers I happened to glimpse from time to time—having been spared the vast bulk of it all, I'm sure.

Be that as it may, as the first of my new collection, the Duesenberg will be installed in the garage bays closest to the Manor which I have had remodeled into a bedroom, after my architects pointed out the structural problems of constructing a ramp up into my former second-floor bedroom and, given the length of the massive automobile, how crowded it would be. The space is easily of a size to accommodate the largest automobiles ever made, as I acquire them one at a time, and as they pass in and out of my bedroom on the way to their permanent home. I am already negotiating for a 1929 Bugatti Royale currently in Japan.

I have ordered the usual number of 1:12 scale Duesenberg models in the hope that you have or soon will find some interest in reviving the happy thought of recovering your collections so impulsively cast off in careless moments of your youth. It wouldn't take much, of course. The merest word spoken over the phone or scribbled on a scrap of paper or even e-mailed might well do it.

Anything, in fact. Anything at all.